I0479920

THE MIDAS CAT

THE DEVIL
WEARS TABBY

TOMMY ELLIS

TOMMY ELLIS

3 SPOT PRESS

PUBLISHED BY

3 SPOT PRESS.

ABOUT THE AUTHOR

Tommy has been a full-time musician and entertainer since 1988 and writes in club-land and holiday park dressing rooms whilst waiting for the bingo to finish. He has played in a nudist camp, has supported some of the biggest names in the music industry and lives with the midas cat and her siblings.

For Jeanette without whose encouragement,
this book would never have been written.

THE MIDAS CAT – PART ONE

The Birthday

CHAPTER 1

Ralph

A midas cat? Of all the things Lauren could have asked for, why a bloody midas cat? The thing was, though, he'd do anything for her, and she damned well knew it! She'd give him one of her Vogue cover-model pouts and almost everything about him would turn to custard. He was sure it was genetic. He even fancied her mum but would never admit it.

Ralph stared through the windscreen at the school-run gridlock, knuckles whitening as he gripped the wheel. His job was to hide things. Usually offshore in places like the Cayman Islands. He was good at it, and the taxman hated him. Finding things like a cat that was so scarce, it hovered between myth and madness was a different matter, though.

Midas cats are rare to the point of legend was what the website *knowyourmidascat* had said. *Child-sized in stature, they blend into the human world almost seamlessly due to their chameleon-like abilities.* So, no worries spotting one then? And to make matters worse, Lauren had asked for the rarest, most valuable version: The tiger-striped one!

Just because Lauren's BFF, Cecily, was bought a Bugatti with personalised plates for her birthday, Lauren had to go one better and had thrown the daddy of all sulks. No sex for a whole month because he'd told her that midas cats go for more than one hundred million on the black market. The fact that there *was* no black market for midas cats because nobody had seen one since the early eighties hadn't smoothed the turbulent waters in the slightest.

There's the website and there's the only known picture of a genuine midas cat. Grainy black-and-white and blurred, it could have been almost anything. A seven-year-old kid in a Dolly Parton wig and gabardine mac or somebody's pet cat in a toupee. Lauren, however, had dug in for the long haul. Sodding midas cat!

The traffic had moved a whole ten feet, when an air-horn blast pulled Ralph back to the present. 'Bugger off,' he muttered. 'Busy.'

The company Mercedes leapt forwards as his foot slipped off the clutch, and the car lurched to a stop. That's when he saw it. A yellow raincoat, ridiculously high heels, and a cigarette holder about three feet long. It couldn't be, could it? He closed his eyes and counted to five before opening them again. Stumbling down the steps of The Dog and Partridge was... 'A bloody midas cat!'

Ralph stared, unsure that his brain had sifted, sorted and filed the correct information. Tabby and white face, big glassy green eyes and a can of Special Brew dribbling its contents over a pair of Jimmy Choos.

'Sod work!' said Ralph. 'I've got a present to catch.'

Weaving from wine bar to pub and pub to kebab shop, Ralph trailed the cat all over town until... 'I know where you live.' He'd tracked it all the way to its front door in a leafy suburb. The rarest cat on earth eats doner kebabs and lives in the 'burbs. Seriously? He knew he had to pick his moment, but the problem was the location. What was he going to do? Ring the doorbell, grab the animal when it answered the door and stuff it in the boot of the car? Not in twitchy-curtain land. No. He needed to do research. He needed a plan.

#midascatcollector turned out to be a saddo with an oversized domestic tabby he'd put a dress on, but Wikipedia's entry had given him an idea. *Midas cats are partial to alcohol, cigarettes and the music of eighties pop star, Adam Ant. They are insufferable snobs and love grilled lobster and exclusive parties.*

The house he'd repossessed last week was still

empty and not due back on the market for a fortnight at least. Perfect. A computer-generated invite, some minor DIY and boom! Lauren would
have a midas cat for her birthday. He'd so be in her
good books... and underwear. The thought made
his head swim.

He slipped the black and gold invite through the
creature's letterbox and watched as it flipped over
and over before settling on the doormat. Now he
had work to do.

CHAPTER 2

The Cat

C at opened an eye. Daylight lasered through a gap in the curtains into Cat's face. Cat closed her eye. 'What a night.' She sat up, sending a cascade of empty tins and bottles clattering to the bedroom floor.

Picking her way through kebab wrappers, beer cans and a traffic cone, Cat weaved towards the kitchen. She stopped to examine the traffic cone. Blurred images played out in her head like a slightly out of tune TV channel. The brawl in the town centre she inadvertently started was perfectly clear as was the arrival of the police. It all got a bit fuzzy between getting behind the wheel of the unattended riot van and waking up just now, though.

The *police stop* sign hanging upside-down from the fridge handle dislodged another memory as

Cat reached for a limp slice of pizza. A cop in full riot gear lumbering down the high street whilst waving a plexi-glass shield over his head had seemed amusing at the time, but Cat realised that she could be in serious trouble. 'Oh well.' She shrugged. 'I'm not in jail, so it couldn't have been that serious.'

Cat grinned to herself then wished she hadn't. Her head might not be hung over, but her face was. 'I need a freshener.' She rummaged in her pelt, pulled out a silver hip flask, popped the lid and took a long pull. The over-proof rum slid down Cat's throat and exploded in the pit of her stomach. 'Better,' she muttered, before heading for the front door.

'Bills, bills, double glazing, more bills.' Cat riffled through the doormat's offerings, casting them aside until she reached the final two. 'Hold up.' Cat perched her half-moon specs on the end of her nose. Two invites on the same night. What are the chances?

You are cordially invited to attend the presentation of the Cambridge Institute medal in honour of Professor Yolanda Barnes, PhD, C.A.T., IMDB, and her discovery of the Free Atomic Ratio Trans-atom. Strict black tie.

Cat didn't own a black tie but had better not miss the presentation. Yolanda was, after all, her sister. Cambridge professor and doctor of theoretical quantum physics, Yolanda, or Yoda, as she hated being called, would count on her attendance. But what about the second invite on the same day? She scanned the black and gold card, paused and read it again. An invite to an exclusive lobster party. Exclusive; Cat liked that word. Lobster; an even better word. She read on. Address: Lector House, Bates Lane. (The last house on the left). No riff-raff, no press, no dogs. Special appearance by Adam Ant.

That did it. Cat was a huge Adam Ant fan. She was more than a fan. She was a super-fan. She'd spent the last three weeks writing a letter to her hero but only got as far as *Dear Mister Ant*. Now she didn't even have to finish it as she'd be meeting the swashbuckling star in the flesh.

'Yes!' Cat did a paw-pump. 'My kind of party. Get in!'

CHAPTER 3

Lauren

T he hard brightness of the mid-January day rapidly dimmed as the sun slunk out of sight below the tree line. She was sure Ralph hadn't seen her, and as Lauren pulled into the little layby on Bates Lane, she killed the lights and engine. Cooling metal ticked in the dusky stillness as she stepped out into the darkening chill. *I'm just going to the club.* The waste of oxygen spent more time at his precious club than he did at home. Well, he wasn't at the flecking club tonight, was he?

As she rounded the curve, she saw it. White-washed but greying in the fading light, the famil-iar shape of Lector House squatted at the edge of the forest. She'd seen the pictures on Ralph's laptop. The owner went mad, or something, and Ralph had handled the repossession. She slowed to an uneasy stop. Distant wood smoke and a creeping green damp cut the frost edged evening. Of all the places he could use as a shag-pad, why here? Lauren's breath hitched. Did she see movement at the tree line?

She stared into the gloom. A man-like shape shuffled into the forest. But it wasn't a man, though, was it? It looked more like a hairless ape and certainly moved like one. It couldn't have been Ralph. He didn't move like that. So, what the hell was it? She backed away, not taking her eyes from the sub-human shape. Was it still there? The darkness had swallowed all sign of it. She shook her head. No. There was nothing there. The shadows had ignited her over-active imagination, that's all. She laughed. It sounded edge-of-hysteria nervous. There was no failed experiment running around in the Hertfordshire woods. There was only Ralph bumping uglies with his latest tart inside that damned farmhouse.

This was a stupid idea. If she waited until after her birthday. After being given a midas cat. She could divorce him, clear out the joint account and go back to Mummy and Daddy's in Hampstead.

She turned the key and unlike the many horror films she'd watched, the Beemer's engine thankfully sprang to life.

'Mummy, Daddy, I'm home.' The front door opened onto lily scented Italian marble, glitter-lit by Louis XIV crystal that hung high above the graceful sweep of the staircase.

'Lauren, darling.' A door opened on Lauren's left and Daddy stepped out of a haze of cigar smoke. 'Lovely to see you, my dear.' He kissed her lightly on the cheek before taking a step back. 'Why the grumpy face?'

'It's Ralph.' Lauren threw an exaggerated pout. 'He said he was going to the club, but I followed him. Instead, he went to that farmhouse he repossessed last week.' She slung her arms around Daddy's neck. 'He's seeing another woman. I'm sure of it.' Should she mention the ape-man she'd seen? There'd been no reports of a break-out from the local zoo, so that just left her mind playing tricks on her. No, it must have been her imagination.

'There there, darling.' Daddy gently stroked her hair. 'Have you actually seen this other woman?' Lauren shook her head. 'No. But why lie if he's not having an affair?'

'Sweetheart, I'm sure there's a reasonable explanation. With vacant properties there's always a risk of vandals, squatters and worse. He's probably just checking it over to make sure it's secure before going on to his club.'
Lauren nodded. It did make sense but even so, he'd promised her a midas cat for her birthday, and if he was busying himself with work, he wasn't tracking down her present. 'I'm still not going back to him until he gets me my very own midas cat, though.'

Daddy gently placed a hand on her shoulder. 'You're set on that, aren't you?'

'Well, Cecily got a Bugatti Veyron for her birthday, and an Indian diamond set in a Welsh gold ring, so why shouldn't I have an exclusive present as well?'

'Oh, Lauren,' said Daddy. 'Midas cats are beyond exclusive. They are so rare; they're thought to be extinct.'

Lauren stamped her foot. No, they weren't extinct. She'd googled it. 'I've read about them online,' she said. 'There's a picture of one and everything. They eat lobster and listen to Adam Ant.'

'Adam Ant?' Daddy smiled briefly. 'I used to listen to Adam Ant.' His smile faded. 'Midas cats are trouble. Big trouble. The last one I heard about was when I was a young boy in the early seventies. Your grandad knew somebody who was after one and it drove this poor soul to murder.'

Lauren opened her mouth to say that she didn't care, but Daddy held up a hand.

'Hear me out,' he said. 'Then decide if a talking cat is really worth it.'

She nodded. Granddaddy knew a midas cat hunter. How cool was that?

'This chap had gambling debts right up to the wazoo, and he was friends with a man who owned a menagerie.'

All Lauren could think about was Granddaddy and the midas cat. How comes she'd never heard this story before?

'The zoo owner offered to clear the chap's debts if he caught him a midas cat for his animal collection. Catch a cat and clear hundreds of thousands. The hunt was on, but the stakes were far higher than anticipated.'

Lauren frowned. 'What do you mean?'

'I'm getting to that,' he said. 'Patience, my girl. Anyway, the hunt didn't go well.'

'Why not?'

'Marc Bolan.'

'Marc Bolan?' Lauren had lost the thread.

'Yes,' said Daddy. 'Back then the midas cat would play cassette tapes of T Rex constantly at full volume, but of course T Rex was on the radio and TV a lot, so when the midas cat hunter heard *Telegram Sam* playing on his kid's nanny's radio, he burst in demanding to know where the cat was, and when she denied all knowledge, he battered her to death in a fit of psychotic rage.'

'He what?' This story had just taken a gruesome turn. 'What happened to Granddaddy's friend?'

'Your granddaddy thinks the midas cat had something to do with it. Without proof, though, nobody can be completely sure, but Lord Lucan hasn't been seen since.'

Everybody in society knew about *Lucky Lucan*. Ordinary people had probably heard of him as well, but she was sure that very few people had heard about the midas cat. 'How comes the midas cat never made the news?'

'Oh, that's easy,' said Daddy. 'The right connections, of course.'

Just wait until Cecily hears about this. The midas cat had family connections, and it caused a murder and a disappearance. She pulled the phone from her jeans pocket. 'I'm going out,' she said as she sent the text.

CHAPTER 4

Ralph

I t had been a long day but rewarding. The invite was sent and according to *knowyourmidascat.com,* Adam Ant, lobster and the word *exclusive* should bring the cat running. The house was rigged and now all Ralph had to do was wait. He pulled the zipper across the mouth of the mask. With its matt black finish, the full body suit was perfect for becoming one with the shadows. The rings connecting to the hooks and chains had to be taped down to stop any rattling. That wasn't usually a problem as the outfit was only ever used at the club. Membership was expensive, but discretion was guaranteed. His platinum card, however, had been temporarily revoked pending an investigation involving a misunderstanding regarding a packet of chilli powder and a posing pouch.

As he did a final exterior check, the smooth note of a BMW engine floated on the still air. Lauren? It couldn't be, could it? If she saw him dressed like this, she'd go scorched earth on him, even if he *was* trying to catch her birthday present.

He darted for the darkening tree line and hoped it either wasn't her, or she'd just turn around and leave when she saw how creepy this place was. It wasn't as if he could take the damned outfit off, as greeting his beloved in a leather thong would gain him nothing but frostbite and a divorce.

The clack of heels on frozen tarmac turned to a crunch as Lauren stepped onto the gravel driveway. Ralph barely dared to breathe in case his fogging breath gave his position away. She was scanning the trees. She was staring straight at him. Any second now she'd bark his name and he'd have no choice but to fess up to his proclivities. His marriage would be over. He shuffled deeper into the trees and waited to hear his name screamed into the dusk, but all he heard were retreating footsteps. He exhaled and shivered as the Beemer rumbled away into the encroaching night.

As his pulse dropped out of the heart attack zone, he began to wonder how she'd found out about Lector House. His mind backtracked. The old man. He'd been mooching around outside their home. Now he gave it some proper thought, he realised just how incongruous it was. The morning he'd gone back for his computer, he was certain he'd closed and locked the back door. Or was he? It was swinging in the cold breeze that lanced the centrally heated air, his laptop open on the coffee table. He'd paid it no mind at the time, closed it up and headed straight for the office.

Hindsight is such a marvellous thing. Details of Lector House had folded out of sight when he'd snapped the laptop shut. Lauren's father. He always said he knew people. The old git was probably some ex cold war spy *Daddy* had sent. Well, so long as he didn't find details of the club, it didn't matter too much. Whatever he'd told Lauren would be forgotten in the blink of an eye, a blink of a midas cat's eye, when he presented her with her very own talking cat.

He slipped behind the bush by the front door. From there he had a perfect view of the first, and hopefully only, trap. The cat would arrive, ring the doorbell, get struck by the GHB tipped dart and pow! Lauren would have her very own midas cat. Elegantly simple. What could possibly...? No, he mustn't even think the word. That was bound to curse the mission.

He breathed in deeply, the smell of leather and sweat calming his zinging nerves. His rapid pulse slowed to a less manic rhythm. It wouldn't be long now. He was sure of it.

He heard the taxi long before he could see it. The clattering rumble of a high mileage diesel engine drifted on the thick fog that had descended. Headlights speared the gloom as the car rounded the bend. This was it. Game on. He could barely control himself as the cat tottered across the gravel on its stupid high heels. A cigarette flared as the animal took a long drag and jetted smoke out of its nostrils. What was the stupid creature wearing on its head? A 1920s flapper hat? What on earth did it think it looked like? He suppressed a giggle without much success and snorted down his nose.

The cat froze, looked up and then over at the bush he was crouched behind. He'd blown it. He stared at the cat, his heart thumpa-thumpa-thumping. The cat stared back; its big glassy green eyes impossible to read in the gloom. A line of icy sweat traced an uncomfortable path down the centre of Ralph's back and he bit down on a shudder. The cat blinked, shrugged and bimbled up to the front door.

Here we go, thought Ralph as the cat reached a paw for the doorbell. Ralph got slowly to his feet in readiness to catch the unconscious feline and watched as the cat's cigarette fell from the end of its *Lady Penelope* holder. A paw pressed the bell. Ralph's pulse revved hard as the cat bent to retrieve the fag from the doorstep. *Thwip!* A sharp pain dug into the centre of Ralph's forehead, followed by light-headedness. Then everything went black.

CHAPTER 5

The Cat

The bright lights of the city had been left far behind and Cat looked out onto darkening fields and hedgerows. The black cab had been travelling for hours. At least that was what it felt like to Cat. Desperate to get the party started, Cat riffled through her handbag until she found her hipflask. She popped the lid and paused. Who was that mad woman outside the pub in Hampstead? When the taxi stopped at the roadworks, the stupid human had stared Cat straight in the face. She'd dropped her fag, and as the cab pulled away, she'd run down the street after it, screaming something about a birthday present or some such drivel. 'Bonkers,' muttered Cat and took a long pull of single malt.

The cab driver leaned over the seat. 'Do what?' Cat was sick of the flat-capped moron's inane jabber.

'United did a sterling job against City in last night's derby.'

So fucking what? Cat made a point of stuffing in her earbuds and staring out of the window. Peasant! At least there won't be any of that sort at the exclusive lobster party. Lobster, mmm. Adam Ant, mmm.

'We're here,' said the cabbie. 'That'll be seventy-five quid.'

Cat dropped a bundle of notes into the driver's outstretched palm and exited the cab. She wasted no time in lighting up a Bensons and screwing it into the end of the Lady Penelope cigarette holder. *Sophisticated? Elegant? Why of course*, thought Cat as she took a drag and fired a stream of smoke out of her nose.

Gravel crunched under her heels as she tottered up the drive to the front door. The house could have been white, but in the fading light Cat couldn't be sure, and wasn't that top window boarded up?

Cat froze as a muffled snort came from the bush by the porch. She scanned the evergreen foliage which looked black in the failing light. Nothing moved. *Must have imagined it.* Cat blinked, shrugged and continued to the door. She reached up to push the doorbell just as the cigarette tumbled from its holder, showering orange sparks as it hit the ground.

Pushing the buzzer, she bent and scooped up the fag in one fluid movement. *Thwip!* Cat frowned. There was a low grunt from the bush followed by a dull thud. *Someone's well pissed,* thought Cat as the door swung silently inwards.

CHAPTER 6

Lauren

'So, you suspect Ralph's having an affair and using the repossessed farmhouse as a... what did you call it again? A shag-pad?'

'Yes, and it gets worse.' Lauren stared at Cecily over the rim of her wine glass.

'What can be worse than that?'

'My birthday present had something to do with a disappearance and a murder.'

Cecily lowered her martini without taking a drink. 'Are you serious?'

'As a plane crash.' Lauren drained her glass. 'I need another drink.'

'That's your fifth.' Cecily tutted. 'You drove here tonight. You're already well over the limit.'

'Well, another won't do me any more harm, will it?'

'Look,' said Cecily. 'Just ease up a bit and tell me about this murder. This is far juicier than the usual diet of babies, affairs and divorces.'

'I suppose it is, really. Anyway, the present I asked Ralph to get me this year is a midas cat.'

'Whoa,' said Cecily. 'That's, like, mega rare and twice as expensive. Can he afford one?'

'He'd blinking well better or all bedroom aerobics will go on hold indefinitely.'

Cecily giggled.

'Anyway,' said Lauren. 'The midas cat was involved... Or should I say Lord Lucan was involved with the midas cat.'

'What, for real?' Cecily reached for her glass. 'This is beyond juicy.'

Lauren recounted the story.

'Let's pop out for a fag.' Cecily pulled a lighter from her bag. 'I need a few minutes to digest this.'

'These roadworks have been going on forever,' said Lauren. The cigarette flared as she pulled hard on it. She savoured the nicotine hit. Ralph hated smoking. Well, she hated Ralph having an affair, so what was he going to do about it? Divorce her? He wouldn't dare!

'That's mental.'

'What?' Cecily had said something, but Lauren's attention had been elsewhere.

'The midas cat having something to do with Lucky Lucan. That's plain mental.'

'I can't disagree with you about that.' Lauren

stared at the stationary traffic, not really focusing on anything in particular. The black cab inched forwards. A pointless exercise, as the lights were still red.

In a moment of clarity, she saw it. Out of the smoky drunken haze swam a pair of huge glassy green eyes. Sitting in the back of the taxi, not more than ten feet away, and staring straight at her was the midas cat. 'Holy flecking Jesus on a pogo stick!' The cigarette tumbled from Lauren's open mouth and exploded in firework sparks as it bounced on the pavement.

'What?' said Cecily. 'Where are you going?'

'My birthday present!' Lauren's feet had already started moving without her brain having any-thing to do with it. 'He's had it delivered!'

'What, where?'

The lights had turned green and the cab had picked up speed.

'Where's it going?' This wasn't right. The midas cat wasn't supposed to leave. It was her birthday present. But if Ralph was having an affair, then there was a chance that his bit on the side was getting her present. 'The rotten rascal!' Lauren stamped her foot and watched as the taxi rumbled down the hill, rounded the corner and was lost to sight. 'My birthday present! Mine! Mine! Mine!'

It had left. The world's only talking cat that was meant for her and her alone was being delivered to her husband's girlfriend. What Ralph didn't know, though, was that she knew where it was going. An unguarded moment and an open laptop was all it took. Having been there once already meant finding it again wasn't going to be a major challenge. The flecking shag pad!

'Lauren.' Cecily had caught up with her. 'Are you OK?' She took Lauren's arm.

'Yes. I flipping am now.' She took out her car keys and strode towards her BMW.

CHAPTER 7

Ralph

A deep and steady throb thundered through Ralph's brain. He reached up. A mountainous lump had grown from the back of his skull. 'Ughhhhhh!' He was lying in a bush next to a concrete planter but couldn't for the life of him figure out why. Images of big green eyes floated out of his subconscious. The pieces were all there but wouldn't slot together. It was like looking at a Picasso jigsaw that had been put together in the wrong order.

He sat up and the world tilted at a radical angle. He fought the urge to puke, and when the ground stopped bobbing about on invisible waves, he gingerly touched his forehead. Somebody had injected him between the eyes and left the hypo in. What sick bastard would do such a thing?

Turning the small feathered dart over in his

palm brought an avalanche of memories crashing through the drugged haze. The midas cat. The dart trap and Lauren's birthday. The puzzle pieces re-arranged themselves and clacked together. Due to a stroke of sheer dumb luck, the damned cat had evaded the first trap. 'Sodding midas cat,' grumbled Ralph.

He grabbed the bush in his leather gloved hands and pulled himself upright. He breathed deeply, white lights pulsing at the edge of his vision. The mission to capture the rarest creature on the planet wasn't over. At least he hoped it wasn't over. There were other traps. Other chances to catch himself a lesser-spotted midas cat.

Acid bile rose in his gullet as nausea swept through him. He pulled back the zip on the leather mask and spat. Parmesan scented drool stretched to the gravel leaving a small rancid pool. He redid the zip.

The door hung open and beyond it was the key to his happiness. All he had to do was not blow it. The thought circled in his head. How could he possibly blow it? The design and engineering that had gone into the hallway trap was flawless. Lasers were set at head height. As soon as the cat cut through the first beam, a brick connected to a wire would swing from the ceiling and knock the animal out cold. If the first trap failed due to some unforeseen reason, there were four others exactly the same. Bam, bam, bam, bam! The cat didn't stand a chance.

The soft focus of Ralph's vision sharpened as the drugs gradually wore off. He edged towards the front door. Wasn't that Adam Ant? He was sure he could hear *Prince Charming* drifting from the hallway. What the hell was the stupid feline up to?

His mouth felt as if he'd just woken up after a heavy night on the booze. With his tongue stuck dryly to the roof of his mouth, and the lump on the back of his head beating in time with his pulse, he opened the door just a crack. He peeked in and froze. The midas cat was partial to Adam Ant. That's what *knowyourmidascat.com* had said, but this was ridiculous. The daft bloody animal was only performing the dance to that laughable video. The stupid thing was singing as well! Not that you could call it singing.

Ralph suppressed a chuckle. The pale pink handbag was swinging all the way to the ceiling. All the way to the head-high lasers.

By the time he'd spotted the major flaw in his design, it was too late: Average human height, five feet nine inches. Info from *knowyourmidascat.com*: Midas cats are child-sized in stature.

Ralph's nose exploded in a spray of blood as the first trap detonated, swung over the midas cat's head and blasted Ralph with a direct hit. He staggered through the remaining lasers and watched a tabby tail exit the hallway just before he got slammed by three more house bricks.

CHAPTER 8

The Cat

C at straightened up and pushed the fag back into her Lady Penelope cigarette holder. Would Adam Ant already be here, or would he arrive under police escort once the party was under way? Anticipation about meeting her idol made Cat's whiskers quiver. This was going to be a fabulous night. Pity it was going to be cut short by her sister's presentation. There was no way she could blow the professor out. If she did, the prof would no doubt find a way to pay her back. Yoda's revenge usually took the form of roping her into some lethal experiment or other. That wasn't an option, so she'd better keep a close eye on the time.

Cat stepped across the threshold, her nose twitching. The house had an unlived-in air about it. Fresh paint and the high-tech disco lights that cut bright red lines in the darkened hallway couldn't cover up the underlying note of musky disuse.

She'd heard about parties like these. Celebrities doing unannounced appearances at exclusive gatherings. They'd try out new material on a small audience before going global. Talk about being in with the in crowd. Cool! Cat grinned, put in her ear buds and cranked the volume.

When the first track kicked in, Cat threw a paw in the air, took a deep breath and powered out the lyrics. She loved singing along to Prince Charming, and she was good at it too. 'I bloody love this song!'

Her pale pink handbag swung high, glittering red as it flashed through a laser light. A gentle whooshing breeze ruffled Cat's face fur. *That's what you get for leaving the front door open*, thought Cat as a dull crunch was followed by a percussive beat that sounded like footsteps. *I don't remember all these sound effects,* thought Cat. *Must be an updated remix.* A muffled bass drum beat out a steady rhythm along with a new vocal track reminding Cat of somebody being hit in the face with a house brick. Cat nodded in appreciation. The new version was very 21st century.

The yellow sign at the far end of the corridor flashed on and off metronomically. Cat stared at the pulsing script. The words *Grilled Lobster* were underscored by a solid pink neon arrow that pointed to a door on the left of the passage. 'Chow time,' said Cat to the empty hallway. 'Yes!'

CHAPTER 9

Lauren

The German engine screamed in protest as it redlined. Lauren dropped the clutch and the Beemer fishtailed out of the parking space in a billowing fog of vaporised rubber. She flew through the red light at the roadworks to a discordant orchestra of horns. *Her* midas cat was leaving town. *Her* midas cat was heading for Lector House where Ralph was waiting to present it to whomever he was shagging. Well, she wasn't going to put up with any of that doggie doodie any more. She had her phone with her. She could get photographic evidence of Ralph's affair. That would satisfy any divorce lawyer. Whether there was a serial killer lurking in the bushes or not, she was too hyped up to care.

She reached across to the glove compartment. Where was that flecking phone? She looked up a nanosecond too late. The lights were red, and the old boy had a foot on the road. He was crossing, and she had to be doing at least sixty. 'Oh, fleck and doodie!' She pulled hard on the wheel and stared at the old man in the rear-view mirror. The years hadn't been kind, and he had to be well into his eighties, but the arrogant entitlement showing through the hunted expression was unmistakable. Granddaddy's photo albums had pictures of a far younger Lord Lucan, but Lauren knew it was definitely him. Was he still hunting the midas cat after all these years? If he was, then that made three of them.

She pushed the accelerator to the floor and the car surged as it hit its power band. Out of town and onto quieter roads, she screamed through a box junction.

The strobing blue lights lit the car's interior giving it a surreal high-speed disco effect. She was over the drink-drive limit and pushing a hundred and ten. Would she stop for the police? Daddy had the right connections. Would she fleck! There was a midas cat with her name on it. She wouldn't stop for a nuclear explosion.

CHAPTER 10

Ralph

The zip-up leather mask had done nothing to soften the blows. Ralph undid the zip and stared in horror as three blood-soaked teeth clattered to the floorboards. Straightened, capped and whitened, those teeth had cost good money. His nose must have been smashed to matchwood because every time he breathed in, liquid gurgles accompanied blinding flashes of nasal agony. The brick traps were incredibly effective and would have caught him a way back into Lauren's heart, not to mention knickers if they had been set to the correct height.

He tried to blink away the blood clouding his vision, but his left eye must have been swollen shut under the mask.

The last he saw of the cat was a tail heading for the kitchen, and the second trap. Good! He stepped as lightly as he could towards what he hoped was an unconscious midas cat.

The red beam flashed in his one good eye. Had he miscounted? Was the final trap still primed? If it was, he didn't have time to react as it was set on a hairpin trigger.

The trapdoor flapped open, and the last brick landed in the centre of Ralph's head with a solid clonk.

Why did she have to ask for a midas cat? She could have had any exotic pet. A Bengal tiger would have been less trouble than this.

He got to his knees, his head a jamboree bag of pain. It was just as well he could only see out of one eye. If he had both, he would be seeing double. He crawled the remaining few feet to the kitchen door. The lobster trap was in there. *Knowyourmidascat.com* couldn't have made it plainer. Midas cats love lobster. He gripped the doorframe and, hoping the cat wouldn't spot him, scanned the room. The well-lit kitchen was too much for his battered senses to handle, and he squinted against the painful brightness.

Fluorescent tubes hummed overhead, casting a near shadowless flat white over the scrubbed work surfaces, and the Formica table that took centre stage. The cat was leaning over the table, its stupid extra-long cigarette holder sticking out of its mouth at what Ralph supposed it thought was a jaunty angle. It had plucked the lobster from the plate. Yes! That was all that was needed to activate the canister of sleeping gas hidden inside the hollowed-out shell.

Ralph crept into the kitchen, his one good eye wide with anticipation. He'd redesigned the furniture to give himself plenty of hiding places from which to spring out onto the animal if the gas failed to activate. Get it in a choke hold until it passes out, tie it up and boom! One captured midas cat, and one rekindled love life. He might even be able to introduce Lauren to some of his proclivities. Gently, of course. But having caught her a midas cat, who knows? Anything could be possible.

The tuneless pop song chuntered from the cat's earphones. *Goody two shoes?* It certainly wasn't quality like a Gilbert and Sullivan opera. *I am a modern major general.* Now that's a proper song. He hated pop music, and this meaningless drivel was the worst kind. It had no class. Still, if it meant being able to sneak up behind the dumb creature without it hearing him coming, he supposed he could suffer a crap pop song for a few more seconds.

The cat took its cigarette holder out of its mouth and placed it on the table before dropping the lobster with a clatter.

What was it up to? Ralph ducked in behind the fridge freezer just as the midas cat spun around to face the door. It was shouting about catching a light. It had spotted the disco lights in the living room opposite. Midas cats love to chase moving lights. Any cat loved to chase moving lights. That was because they were all idiots.

Scattered around the room, however, were a dozen bear traps disguised inside hollowed out cuddly toys. Teddy bears with a real bite. Ralph grinned at his own genius. The stupid thing was doomed and didn't even know it.

The cat left the kitchen leaving nothing but the humming light fixture and the hissing gas canister. Ralph stared at the table. The cigarette's glowing tip lined up perfectly with the lobster's head. That was where the gas came out. Now, what *did* that warning label say about explosive gasses and naked flames again?

The bright flash was a fraction quicker than the blast, and Ralph's bowels emptied as the kitchen imploded, burying him under an entire house extension.

CHAPTER 11

The Cat

C at's eyes had adjusted instantly to the kitchen's fluorescent brightness.

Now that was a serious lobster. Sunburnt and resting on a bed of unnaturally green lettuce, it was the biggest Cat had ever seen. It couldn't be real, though? Could it?

Cat rummaged in her handbag for a hipflask, unscrewed the cap and guzzled the entire contents. 'Tia Maria and Redbull. Now *there's* a drink,' she said to the empty kitchen and belched loudly enough to rattle the window frame. Adam Ant's *Goody Two Shoes* flowed down the wires making her ears tingle. Cat loved music, especially the music of Adam Ant. It had class, meaning and best of all it had a kickass dance rhythm.

The lobster was much heavier than Cat had anticipated. That meant it was full of juicy meat.

The first wave of caffeine from the Tia Maria-Redbull mix washed through Cat's system, making her whiskers vibrate. Perfect timing, as the excitement of the day was making her feel a tad drowsy. A pick-me-up was just what she needed. Right now, though, it was chow time. She placed the cigarette holder on the table, picked up the lobster and was about to break off a claw, when a strobing light flashed across her peripheral vision. Her head snapped round, and the lobster slipped from her paws clattering onto the plate. In the living room on the opposite side of the hallway, disco lights cast intermittent spots of colour across the walls and ceiling and scattered across the floor were cuddly toys ripe for shredding.

'Catch the lighty. Fuck, yeah!' She took off across the hall just as *Goody Two Shoes* reached its explosive finale. The Sound effect of cannon fire was so good, it could almost have been in the next room. These updated tracks she'd downloaded were something special. Right now, though, she had more important things to think about. She had lights to catch.

She focussed on the living room wall and picked out a small red dot moving erratically across the peeling wood-chip wallpaper. Her head flicked left and right as her eyes widened to pull in as much light as possible. 'You're mine,' she said.

The alcohol and caffeine aftershock propelled her across the room. Pinging off the light switch, she ricocheted from the ceiling down onto the floor where she bounced off a fluffy teddy bear, sending it hop-skipping across the carpet towards the corridor.

Springing up onto the lighting rig, she pulled a can of Special Brew from her handbag. Malty bubbles frothed as the heavily shaken can fizzed and gurgled. She lifted the can to her lips and stopped. 'The professor's party! Shit!' The can slipped from her grip as she checked her watch. 'I'm going to miss Adam Ant. It's either that or blow out my sister. Oh bugger!'

She leapt from the lighting rig and out through the gap in the back door. 'Better call a cab.'

Just as she was about to dive back into her handbag, blue flashing lights cut through the fog. He'd arrived. Adam Ant was coming down the lane under a police escort, just as she imagined he would. Prince Charming in person. Maybe he'd play some new songs especially for her.

She picked up the pace and skipped up the road as multiple headlights cut through the ice laden mist. Screaming engines and howling sirens shattered the deep quiet as the entourage neared its destination. Adam Ant was nearly here. Cat would get a personal performance as she was the only one who'd bothered to show up.

The cars rounded the curve at a serious speed. Cat focussed on the BMW in front. Mr Ant was bound to be in that one as all the rest were cop cars. There had to be some sort of mistake, though. The loopy blonde woman Cat had seen outside the pub in Hampstead was behind the wheel, and she had a determined expression etched across her features.

That wasn't right. Where was Mr Ant? Cat's eyes locked onto the loopy woman's. Shock and surprise flashed across the woman's face and Cat realised she wouldn't be able to stop in time.

Cat's natural reactions kicked in. The tree was perfectly placed for a vertical take-off and she sprung up the trunk. Even in heels she was an expert climber.

From her branch above the lane, she looked down as the events unfolded below.

CHAPTER 12

Ralph

W hat the hell just happened? Ralph breathed in and barked a dusty cough. Intermittent flickering light illuminated Hiroshima-like devastation.

A plume of water flashed silvery white as it jetted overhead, and firework sparks arced from exposed electrical wiring.

His brain quickly got up to speed. The flammable sleeping gas, the fag, the explosion, the midas cat. It all came down to the bloody midas cat.

He moved his arms. They hurt but moved without screaming agony, which meant they weren't broken. That was a good start. He moved his legs. Also not broken. The only real problem was the lack of feeling from anything below the waist. That *wasn't* a good sign, but at least he wasn't dead. If he was dead, then this was a seriously messed up version of heaven.

He cleared away the worst of the debris and hauled himself into a sitting position. The kitchen extension had gone, replaced by a Tracey Emin bomb-site sculpture.

Standing took a mammoth effort of concentration. He'd discovered that when you can't feel anything from the waist down, it's not that easy to balance.

He patted himself down. He was in one piece, but the backside of the gimp suit had been ripped out. He touched something warm and wet that dribbled out of the tear. He'd shat himself, and it was all that fucking cat's fault. He'd worked so hard trying to capture a unique present for Lauren, and the present goes and bloody nearly kills him.

'Right, that's it!' Something in Ralph's mind broke. He was almost sure he heard the crack. 'She's not getting a midas cat.' He stumbled towards the passageway, temper rising steadily. 'She's getting a midas cat fur coat.' The white-hot anger over-rode all pain. He was going to kill that damned cat.

He reached up to push a flap of torn gimp mask out of his one good eye. The leather felt odd. The mask didn't have hair. It didn't when he'd put it on. It did now, though. The flap slapped back into place with a wet splat, and a spray of blood speckled the side of the fridge. He caught a glimpse of his reflection in a shard of window glass and closed his eye. It was worse than he thought. 'Oh fuck!' He opened his eye again. Busted nose, torn scalp, shattered teeth and blood... Lots of blood. The fucking cat had turned him into an extra from a zombie apocalypse movie.

The bastard animal was in the lounge. All he had to do was go in there and grab it. Teach it a lesson for turning him into Frankenstein's monster's rejected half-brother.

No. He had to calm down. The lounge was full of beartraps. If he went blundering in there, things would only get worse for him. He had to play it cool. He stuck his head around the door.

Flying around the room like a wall-of-death stunt rider was the cat. It barely touched the floor as it bounded and bounced in the pulsing disco-lit living room. What the hell was the idiot up to now?

Ralph's attention wavered as the cat tore around the walls. Something wasn't right. The back door. He'd locked it to stop the midas cat from escaping. He had, hadn't he? If he had, then why was it standing ajar? A darker patch of night moved at the edge of Ralph's vision. There was someone out there. Somebody else knew the midas cat was here, and that somebody had come to steal away his one shot at happiness. He wasn't about to let that happen. Not after all the hard work he'd put in. He'd just have to make a grab for the midas cat before the mystery man did. There was only one way to do it, and that was to do it.

The second he stepped into the living room, he realised his mistake. Didn't he warn himself earlier about this? He did, didn't he?

The teddy-bear he'd stepped on folded in on his left ankle at the same moment the feeling returned to his bottom half. The disguised bear trap that he'd found so amusing bit with an agonising finality.

He stuffed his fist into his mouth to stop himself from screaming, and as he hit the floor, he could see the cat perched on the lighting rig. It was looking at its watch. What the fuck for? It's a bloody cat. Cats don't need to check the time.

That's when he noticed the can of Special Brew. The midas cat had dropped it and the puddle of beer spread in a wide pool across the carpet and soaked the side of Ralph's head. He looked on powerlessly as the cat leapt from the lighting rig out through the back door.

One of the disco lights fired a green beam through the widening gap and lit on the face of the intruder. It was the weird old man who was hanging about his house and he looked familiar. Who the hell was he?

Ralph didn't have time to ponder on this as the lighting system had started to sway. The cat had leapt from the towering rig with such force, it had broken the safety bracket. The high voltage, high powered, electrical equipment fell gracefully into the puddle of Special Brew.

Electricity and beer don't mix. Ralph knew this. *Next year she's getting socks* was Ralph's final thought as the smell of burning hair filled his lungs.

CHAPTER 13

Lauren

The thickening mist did nothing to hide Lauren from the law as she sped on into the country lanes. Trees reached across the road forming an organic tunnel, and the car's headlights picked out a narrowing grey ribbon that vanished into the strobe-lit blue fog.

There had to have been half a dozen cars on her tail now, and it wouldn't surprise her if she heard the heavy thud of rotor blades closing in from above.

None of that mattered, though, as she had an appointment with the midas cat. Besides, Daddy could make all the motoring charges go away.

The right-hand curve was tighter than it looked, and the Beemer's back end stepped out. Metal squealed as the near-side rear wing scraped across dry stone walling, sending up an eruption of sparks.

She looked up and squinted. The rear view was whited out by main beams that had to be three feet from her boot at the most. She swiped at the mirror, popping it free. It clattered across the dashboard and vanished into the passenger footwell.

'Get off my bum, you nutters!'

The road ahead straightened out and Lauren floored the accelerator. The overgrown road sign that read *Bates Lane* flashed by unseen, but she knew it was there. If she could keep up the speed past the layby, the cops wouldn't have any way of passing her. She could block the road and they wouldn't be able to do a damn thing. One last curve, and the midas cat would be hers. The door mirrors told a different story, though. Reality was writ large in the blinding glare of police headlights.

'Flecking doo!' she yelled and looked back at the road ahead. 'Oh shit, it's the fucking midas cat!'

Big glassy green eyes shone from under a 1920s flapper hat. Her birthday present was standing in the middle of the road. She yanked the wheel hard to the right. Standing to one side of the cat with his arms outstretched as if making a grab for it was... 'Oh God, it's Lord Lucan!'

The old man looked up as Lauren stood on the brakes. An oasis of calm clarity slowed time. The car struck the missing Lord with a muffled thud. Lauren wondered if the fog deadened the sound or if that was what running somebody over actually sounded like.

As Lord Lucan's feet disappeared over the car's roof, Lauren's eyes flicked back to the road.

The last thing she saw before the airbag exploded was the massive oak tree. Then everything went black.

CHAPTER 14

The Cat

Cat stared down from her perch. Who was the old bloke in the middle of the road? He must have been right behind her just before she scooted up the tree.

She looked on in morbid fascination. There was no way the old sod would be able to get out of the way in time, as the woman's car must have been doing at least eighty.

The dull thud as the old man was scooped up and over the bonnet was followed by a metal-tearing crunch as the Beemer shook Cat's tree. She dug her claws into the branch, determined not to fall.

'That was well intense,' she muttered to herself as the six police cars pulled to a tyre smoking stop. High viz jackets and dazzling torch light filled the lane as policemen leapt from their cars and rushed to the scene.

Not wishing to be questioned, or indeed, held up in any way, Cat bounded from her branch down into the neighbouring field out of sight of the police. If she called a cab, she'd be spotted, and there was no way she was walking all the way to Cambridge from here.

There were, however, six unoccupied police cars not, at present, being used by anyone. They didn't need all six. Surely, they wouldn't miss one if she borrowed it for the night.

Slipping in behind the wheel, she adjusted the seat and executed a perfect three-point turn.

THE MIDAS CAT
– PART TWO

The Cambridge Institute Lectures

CHAPTER 1

Ralph

The old man lurking outside his house was definitely Lord Lucan. Lurking. That was the proper name for it.

Ever since he had been discharged from hospital, he couldn't stop thinking about... about... Oh, what was his bloody name again?

Ralph's mind skipped like a dysfunctional CD player. The painkillers the doctor had given him turned his tight intellect to custard. He'd read the info sheet: Do not drive. Do not operate heavy machinery. Side effects included the possibility of hallucinations.

Fucking great! Stumbling around Asda, tripping his tits off, talking to an imaginary friend whilst rummaging in the bargain bin.

He got to his feet. Or more accurately, he got to his foot. His left foot couldn't be saved and had been replaced with a temporary prosthesis. His right foot was a size nine, and his left foot was, for the time being at least, a size thirteen. If he didn't concentrate, he tended to walk around in circles.

All this shit because Lauren had wanted... No, wanted wasn't a strong enough word. Insisted? Demanded was about right. Yes. She'd demanded he get her the rarest cat on earth as a birthday present.

As he reached for the bottle of pills on the scarred coffee table, his brain jumped back to where it was supposed to be. Lord Lucan had broken into his house. Of that he was more than sure. It wasn't his house anymore, though, was it? The divorce had cost him everything. Her richer-than-Trump father had seen to that. Spousal abuse? He'd never laid a finger on her, so where had the black eyes and bruising come from?

He dry-swallowed a painkiller and his face tightened in disgust. Still, look on the bright side, eh? That was what his solicitor had told him. What bloody bright side? A ten-year stretch for a crime he didn't commit, have his name on the sex offenders register, and be some convict's beatch, or give Lauren the house, the car, all their joint savings and a twenty-grand fine for mental cruelty. He so wanted to be arrested for a crime he *did* commit and beating up a lawyer was just the thing, but he could barely stand up straight, let alone throw an accurate punch.

He stumbled into the bathroom and stared

at the bandaged creature in the cracked mirror. Today was the day. The bindings were coming off, and he would see what the healing process had left behind.

He peeled away the wrappings without blinking. 'Oh, God that's scary.' Scars criss-crossed his head where the scalp had been re-attached, and hair sprouted in random clumps like weeds in a derelict car park. He scanned the rest of his face and tried not to wince. His re-built nose was, as the surgeon said, only temporary, but the best they could do when factoring in the budgetary restraints. It worked, sure. He could breathe and almost smell. The problem was, well... It was a misshapen lump of galvanised black rubber. In the middle of his face was a scaled down piece of lorry tyre with holes drilled in it for nostrils. If it said "Dunlop" on the outside rim, he wouldn't be surprised.

He slotted the second-hand dentures into place before taking a long hard look at the disturbing thing in the mirror.

What had they done? Gone down the local scrapyard and bought a skip-load of knocked-off spares? Jesus! He was an escapee from a zombie apocalypse movie and was sure to end up sitting on a park bench in the church yard nursing a bottle-shaped bag and arguing with himself.

So, it had come down to this. Out on police bail, and into temporary accommodation with his temporary foot, and his temporary nose, living his temporary life.

Due to the present financial climate, we regret to inform you... That was how the letter began. No wife, no home and now, no job.

That was two months ago, and as he stood in the bathroom of the unheated flat listening to the barking dog next door, and the permanently mewling baby above, his resolve solidified into something he could almost touch. He may never get his old job back, but this year, somehow, he was going to win Lauren back. Whatever it took, no matter how unpleasant, he was going to do it.

The letterbox flapped, and a muffled thomp sounded from the doormat. He'd learnt to listen out for the different sounds. Letters, bills, junk-mail, and the local free paper. This was definitely the Weekly Echo and not dogshit wrapped in newspaper. If he ever got his hands on those bastard kids...

He limped down the hall, scooped up the paper and skimmed the headlines: *This year's Cambridge Institute Lectures to be hosted by a cat.* His interest was piqued. He'd heard about this. The only Cambridge professor in history to be a cat. An actual domesticated feline.

He didn't feel the loose sofa spring spear his backside as he flopped onto the settee: *Nobel Prize winning cat, Professor Yolanda Barnes is set to host this year's Cambridge Institute lecture. A controversial move, considering the events of last year's London*

Royal Society lecture.

The article niggled him. It was important for some reason, but he just couldn't pin down why.

Professor Barnes, Ph.D., C.A.T., I.m.d.b., sister of the only lesser spotted midas cat in existence, is said to be thrilled to host this prestigious event.

Ralph dropped the newspaper into his lap and didn't even notice. 'That's it!' he shouted and was answered by a battery of yapping and sleep-killing baby screams. He didn't care. He was getting his wife and his life back, so the barking bloody dog, the howling poxy baby, and the evil sodding kids could all die of an incurable tropical blood disorder as far as he was concerned.

He was going to catch himself a midas cat, and this cat-professor was going to help him do it!

CHAPTER 2

The Cat

C at fumbled in her handbag. 'Where are my bloody keys? I'm sure they're in here somewhere.' Her paw pushed aside casino chips, chip shop chips, an empty hip-flask, and a large pink zippo.

'Oh, here we are.' Cat Staggered slightly on her glittery gold heels and aimed the key at the lock. After two failed attempts, she squeezed one eye shut and leaned into the keyhole. 'Bullseye.' The lock turned, the door swung inwards, and the momentum propelled Cat into the hallway where she face-planted a large terra-cotta pot. She shook her head, dirt flying from the ends of her whiskers, before she turned to close the door.

A pale rosy glow silhouetted the rooftops to the east and the late winter frost shone in myriad sparkles.

It had been a good night. Pub, club, casino, and then everything went a bit fuzzy around the edges.

There was something about busting some moves on the casino roof, blowing a raspberry at the fireman when he got to the top of his ladder and using her Dolly Parton wig as a parachute.

Cat grinned to herself before noticing a small golden card on the doormat. 'What do we have here?' Focussing hard through the drunken haze, she scanned the print: *You are cordially invited to attend this year's Cambridge Institute Lecture. This year's visiting lecturer – Professor Y Barnes, Ph.D., C.A.T., I.m.d.b.*

Cat re-read the card. Her sister Yolanda was a brainiac of the highest order and the inventor of a device that could have had untold potential. The demonstration of the Atomic Re-configuring Size Expander at Oxford University had been a hoot. Their brother Jimmy had strict instructions. She remembered them vividly. *Green button for size expansion and red button for size reduction.*

Cat didn't have a clue that Jimmy could only see in black and white. And how was she to know the lab was a no smoking area? Science labs were always places of bangs, flashes and funny smelling smoke.

If her brother hadn't put his tail right where she was stubbing her fag out, he wouldn't have swung the beam activator and shrunk Oxford's head of experimental physics to the size of a hamster.

Still, it was good fun trying to catch him, even if it meant Yolanda would never get invited back to Oxford as a guest professor ever again.

Was she going to attend the lecture? Hell, yeah!

CHAPTER 3

The Professor

'**N**ow, where did I put? Ah yes, here it is. Twenty grams. No. Better make it fifty. The kids will want to see a big bang after they've mixed the gunpowder.'

The subdued lighting in the Cambridge University lab glinted off test tubes, Bunsen burners, and all manner of scientific looking gadgets and instruments.

Professor Yolanda Barnes leaned back in her chair, stretched and yawned widely. Preparations were nearly complete for the first part of the lecture. She allowed herself a small smile. Hosting the Cambridge Institute Lectures was a real honour. She'd be following in the footsteps of Newton, Einstein and Voltaire and had the chance to inspire young minds, not to mention making a few of them jump with loud explosions.

She also had a chance to redeem herself after last year's Boxing Day Lecture. A talk about theoretical quantum physics and the possibility of time travel. The mocked-up time machine built around her own time resonance theory looked amazing. Polished brass, flashing dials and the world's only fully functioning worm-hole generator. Untested, but so long as it remained unplugged, it shouldn't have caused any problems.

The plan was simple enough. A volunteer from the audience would sit in the button-down leather seat, pull the brass lever, and a 3-D projector would give the impression of the auditorium going back in time. Turn up the house lights and the kid magically re appears in the present having, in actuality, gone nowhere at all.

The weak point in the plan, however, was getting her sister, Cat, to plug in the projector. The special effects were far better than during the rehearsal and much more realistic. The 21st century energy saving lights became jaundiced tungsten filament bulbs that flickered and died as wartime bombs rained down. Fashion regressed to starched collars and top hats as plastic gave way to wood panelling and dancing gas flames.

When the lights came up, the kid was nowhere to be seen. Did she know where he was? When Yolanda discovered that Cat had plugged in the worm-hole generator instead of the 3-D projector, not only could she not say with any certainty *where* he was, she couldn't be entirely sure *when* he was.

A swift online search soon solved the problem, however. The kid had played a pivotal role in The Battle of the Somme and married his great-great-grandmother in 1920. The bloody time machine actually worked, but she'd never be able to admit it. If she went back and retrieved him, he would never have been born in the first place and wouldn't have travelled back in time to marry his great-great grandmother which would mean that he wouldn't have been born in the first place, which meant...

She slumped back in her chair. Time paradox always gave her a headache. Still, what could possibly go wrong with a lecture entitled *the explosive nature of chemicals?*

CHAPTER 4

Ralph

R alph stared at the water stained ceiling, then back at the computer screen. No, it hadn't changed. He looked up again. If he focussed hard enough on the mutant Isle of Wight shaped smudge, maybe, just maybe, the info would be different the next time he looked down at the laptop. Yeah, right. Would it bog-roll! Tickets for the Cambridge Institute Lectures were for 8 to 15-year-olds only, and it had been a long time since Ralph had seen teen-hood.

He paced around the flat, nose-blind to the mushroomy dereliction. There had to be a way into the bloody institute. Other than the obvious flaw, the plan was brilliant. Go to the lecture, kidnap the professor and ransom her for her sister. One midas cat, one revived marriage. Simples!

His problem was not being 8 to 15 years old.

He stopped pace-limping and glanced absently at his tattered gimp-suit hanging by the door. It had been the perfect outfit down at the club. He could indulge his proclivities to the fullest, and nobody would know who he was. Good times.

He turned away to continue pacing but stopped when the spark of an idea glimmered at the back of his medication-fogged mind. The gimp-suit with its torn leather mask and ripped backside held the key to success, but what the hell was it?

The bawling infant in the flat above him faded to a background hum as he cast his line into the memory pond and waited for a bite. The idea was there. It just needed teasing out. His focus narrowed as the circuits in his head sparked and crackled. Nobody knew it was him at the club be-cause… Why?

He'd stopped breathing and hadn't noticed, and his fake foot hovered above the sticky grey carpet. Nobody knew it was him at the club because he was in disguise. That's why!

He breathed in and the oxygen-rush made the room spin. He gripped the back of the sofa as the plan filled his mind. Damn! Was he a genius, or what?

Ralph could feel the checkout girl's eyes on him as he rummaged in his wallet. When you didn't have a kid with you, buying a school uniform was seriously embarrassing. He knew he should have bought it online. The downside with eBay, though, was not being able to try it on, and at least Asda had changing rooms.

The mother with the 7-year-old boy had been a hair away from screaming the place down when she opened his cubicle curtain by mistake. Seeing a fully-grown man in shorts, long socks, school cap and tie wasn't an everyday occurrence. Especially when the man had a mutant nose, one foot bigger than the other and someone else's dentures. School disco themed fancy-dress party was an inspired excuse, but the mother still hauled the kid out of there sharpish.

'That'll be £87.50, please.'

'What?' The checkout girl had said something, but he'd been too engrossed in the changing-room episode to hear what it was. What was it again? Oh yes. Money. He handed his debit card over and hoped he was still in the black as he tried not to make eye contact.

It was one of those days when the drizzle was so fine, it seemed to defy gravity and go up as well as down. Ralph hadn't noticed the drenching mist until he was inside the university. The trail of drips was a dead give-away. He had to dry off. He shook the water from his cap and wrung the mop-head wig out into the sink before popping three more painkillers. He grimaced. Anything tasting that bad had to be doing him some good, surely?

As easy as it was getting in, he didn't want to get caught now. How could he explain away a pocket of fresh prawns, and a bottle of horse tranquiliser?

The mop took way too long to get back on straight. If somebody needed to use the toilet, he'd be well busted. He scrunched the cap onto the Bissell Eezee-squeeze and froze. Hollow footsteps echoed in the corridor. If he hid in one of the cubicles, would he get caught? In the movies, the bad guy always looks under the toilet door or just fires half a dozen bullets through it.

What was he thinking? Cambridge University caretakers don't carry guns. At least, he hoped they didn't.

The footsteps stopped outside the door. If he hadn't dithered and flapped for so damned long, he'd have been in and out and back in the queue of kids waiting for the doors to open instead of trapped in this loo, waiting to get caught.

The handle clunked down, and the door screeched open on unoiled hinges. If he made a dash for the cubicles now, he'd never make it without a shitload of noise. There was only one thing for it. He eased backwards towards the urinals, not taking his eyes from the door. If he pretended to be having a piss, he could say he had to go, or he'd have wet himself. He was supposed to be 9-years-old, after all.

The hinges squealed and then stopped. Ralph stood at the urinal, heart trip-hammering in his chest. In a room full of people, he could just about pull off the disguise. In an empty uni toilet, he had no chance unless the janitor was blind or stupid.

He looked over his shoulder. The door was half open and muttering drifted from the other side.

'Better sort these hinges out.' The caretaker was talking to himself. Why didn't he bugger off and hold the conversation somewhere else? He might get better reception.

'A can of WD40 should do it.'

Yes, well, thought Ralph. *Sod off and get one and leave me to get on with my bloody kidnapping in peace.*

The door let out one last dry scream before closing with a thomp.

'They'd better be paying me overtime for this.' The muttering followed the fading footsteps up the corridor.

This was it. He had to go now or the lowlife blue-collar knobhead would catch him with enough ketamine to floor a whole herd of stampeding football supporters.

Professor Yolanda Barnes. Ph.D., C.A.T., I.m.d.b. Gold lettering stood out against the dark oak. This was the place. He put his ear to the cool wood and held his breath. The deep sonorous ticking of a large clock and his own racing pulse thundering in his temples were the only sounds. Nobody talking and nothing moving.

If there was anybody in the office, he could always say he'd got lost looking for the toilet. No. Sod that! He was here to kidnap the professor, and this was the professor's office. If there was anybody in the office, it was bound to be who? Well, duh!

He had prawns. He had ketamine. All he had to do was get the cat to eat some seafood, wait for it to pass out and... And what? Lug it through the corridors of Cambridge University in a fireman's carry? A bit suspect didn't quite cover it. OK, he'd got in through the fire escape and would get out that way once the deed was done, but he hadn't thought it through, had he?

He swallowed three more painkillers just to take the edge off and reached a trembling hand for the polished brass doorknob. This was it. He was really going through with it. On the far side was his shot at a second chance. Top drawer banking job, six-bedroomed house in a gated community, company Merc and regular and, of course, irregular sex. Not much to play for, then?

The room was exactly how he imagined a college don's chambers to look like. The ticking issued from the full-sized long case clock. 'Whoa, that's pricey,' he whispered to himself.

A single green-shaded desk lamp gave the floor-to-ceiling bookcases a muted glow. Huxley, Shakespeare, Dickens, Chaucer, Blyton. Classics!

Ralph's curiosity over-rode his urgency to leave the drugged prawns and escape. He plucked professor Hawking's book, *A Brief History of Time* from the shelf and opened it to the flyleaf. A neat thumbprint sat beneath the typed legend. *To my dear friend Yolanda.*

He ran a finger over the spines and pulled out

a hand-bound original manuscript of *Harry Potter and the Philosopher's Stone*. Signed, of course. In another life he would have got on well with the animal.

He fumbled in his pockets. Bone china plate stolen from Oxfam, Shelled king-prawns shop-lifted from Lidl, and a bottle of ketamine from his days at the club.

Last prawn injected; he froze. He knew he shouldn't have wasted time checking out the literary collection. By the sound of things, the bloody caretaker was back. Wasn't he supposed to be fixing the squeaky bog door? What the fuck was he doing outside the prof's office?

'Help the professor with her experiments. Take the professor a plate of prawns.' The familiar nasally whine of the janitor came from right outside the door. 'Next thing they'll want me to do will be to wipe the professor's furry arse. Well, they can go and kiss my hairy one.'

There was no getting away with it this time. The moron was coming in, and he had to hide. He scanned the room. There had to be somewhere. There were two other doors. Two doors meant two chances.

Ralph's inner voice spoke up, and for some bizarre reason it sounded like a cheesy seventies game-show host. What a time for the painkillers' side effects to kick in. Red traffic lights when you're in a hurry, adverts when you turn on the telly, and now this shit!

'Ralph Williams, welcome to *Hide or Die*. This is your last chance to see Lauren naked. All you have to do is choose door A, B or C.'

The first door led back to the corridor where the caretaker was, so that was a non-starter.

'Do you want to phone a friend, Ralph? Well, too bad. It looks like you haven't got any.' The head-voice drilled into his resolve. He had to figure this out and soon.

'I'll give you a clue. Door B leads to the roof, Ralph. Do you really want to go that way?'

Did he? He didn't have a clue.

'What about door C, Ralph? Could that be the correct exit?'

What was door C, a cupboard?

'Better hurry, Ralph. Remember, in *Hide or Die* you can either hide or... Yep, you guessed it.'

Shit or bust, he'd better go for it. 'I'll take door C, thanks.'

The darkness was almost complete apart from a faint greenish outline around the frame. When he'd glanced into the cupboard, he couldn't believe how stuffed it was. Boxes brimmed over with paperwork, dismembered robotics, and what he surmised to be failed experiments.

He pushed a box of test tubes to one side and cringed when they tinkled. Squeezing into the space left no margin for error. If he moved even a fraction, something was bound to make a shedful of noise.

'I'm supposed to be a caretaker, not some brainiac's lackey.' The old boy shuffled around the office wheezing like an asthmatic steam engine.

'I don't remember putting these prawns in here. Was I in here earlier, or not? Oh, I'm buggered if I know.'

If Ralph got caught, it looked like it wouldn't matter. He could commit a murder in front of the janitor and get away with it. The senile old fuck!

'Bloody kids!' The wheezy old fart hog-snorted before hocking up a wet, bubbling cough. 'Bringing a water-pistol to a serious scientific lecture! This is Cambridge, not some council-run comprehensive. Scumbags, the lot of 'em.'

Ralph's left foot had started itching. He'd read about phantom limb pain, but this was worse than he could ever have imagined. Millions of tiny insects crawled under the surface of a non-existent foot. He wanted to tear the skin off, but that had been incinerated weeks ago.

'Hey, folks!' Mister Smarmy-Gameshow-Host had to appear now, didn't he! 'We've raised the stakes by giving our contestant an itch in an amputated body part.'

Yeah, thought Ralph. *You had to, didn't you. Thanks a pantsful, you evil fucker.*

'Stay tuned to find out if he can keep quiet long enough not to get caught.'

Ralph's left leg had started jiggling on its own accord as if it was trying to stop the crawling flesh all by itself.

Thump. Thump, thump! He gripped his leg in

both hands. If he didn't stop kicking the door, Gomash, or whatever his bloody name was, would open it, and he'd be more screwed than a screw at a screw makers' convention.

'Wassat?' Shuffling footsteps came nearer and nearer. *He we go,* thought Ralph. *Game over.*

'Looks like our contestant is about to take the walk of shame, folks.'

'Oh, do shut up, you cheesy bastard,' Ralph muttered under his breath.

The door swung open and Ralph froze, unable to think of anything else to do. A brown hardware shop-worker's coat hung limply from a hunched, bony frame, and a pair of faded-denim coloured eyes stared owlishly and hugely magnified through the thickest glasses Ralph had ever seen. If the old sod stood in direct sunlight, he'd catch fire.

Ralph stood motionless, barely daring to breathe as the janitor stared hard at him.

'Jesus, that's one ugly mannikin!' Gomash grimaced, his face folding in on itself just as he swung the door shut. 'God knows what the professor's up to now.' Footsteps followed a hacking cough across the room, and the outer door clicked shut. Ralph breathed out.

'Give our contestant a big hand for making it through to the next round!' Applause filled Ralph's head, and he found that he was smiling broadly. Yes, he *had* got through to the next round. He picked the water pistol from the desk and studied it carefully. Cats hate water. His smile widened further. He was now armed!

The drizzle had stopped by the time he re-joined the back of the queue. It was just as well, really, as he didn't want the mop-head wig soaking up a gallon of rain, only to empty its contents down the back of his neck.

He nodded to himself. He'd set the trap, so that meant all he had to do now was enjoy the show and pop backstage afterwards to collect the unconscious professor. Then he could move onto part two of the plan. Kidnapping was so delightfully old school.

He squeezed in to the kid-sized seat and waited for the hall to fill up.

CHAPTER 5

The Cat

'Err, let me see, now.' Cat pushed aside the pink zippo and delved deeper into her handbag. 'Ah, here we are.' She perched the wire rimmed half-moon spectacles on the end of her nose and studied the ticket. 'Row two, seat one.' She looked at the allocated seat, then back at the ticket. 'Seriously?' There had to have been a cock-up on a scale that would necessitate government intervention, as sitting in the seat directly in front of Cat was the biggest kid in the entire lecture theatre.

'Trust me to get stuck behind fat-head.' Cat thrust her specs back into her handbag and sat down. 'I won't be able to see a sodding thing.'

Cat stared hard at the kid. What was wrong with its hair? Beneath an under-sized school cap was what looked like the head of a mop. Industrial-strength strands flopped lifelessly over the woollen blazer's collar. Why was the idiot wearing a floor cleaner on his head?

The kid kept glancing to the right of the stage as if he was looking for someone, and Cat caught a side-on view of his nose. Not only was the kid fat and ugly, he was no doubt riddled with some sort of highly contagious disease. Cat shuddered, whiskers vibrating with repulsion. The misshapen snout looked as though it was infected with a rare tropical fungus.

Cat dipped back into her handbag, paw closing around the smooth curves of the hipflask. 'This'll keep the doctor away.' She took along pull and smacked her lips as the single malt traced a fiery path down her throat.

As Cat settled in, she soon realised the view of the stage was, to say the least, compromised. She craned left and right. She even tried stretching up to peer over the top, but it was no use. All Cat could see was a tiny fraction of the stage and a green school cap perched on top of a mutant hairdo that framed an almost perfectly round head. Bloody typical!

The lights dimmed, and the background chatter dropped to an expectant silence. A bright white spotlight flared, and there on stage stood a small black cat with huge green eyes. Its black cape billowed as it stepped forwards. 'Good evening, boys and girls, and welcome to this year's Cambridge

Institute lecture.' The applause filling the auditorium quickly died away as the cat on the stage introduced herself. 'My name is Professor Yolanda Barnes, and tonight's lecture is entitled the explosive nature of chemicals. Some chemicals look, smell and even feel identical but behave in radically different ways.'

Cat wriggled and squirmed to try to gain a clearer view, but whatever she did only made matters worse. Fat-head's blockade was now total. Cat's vision of the stage was now precisely nil.

'In the green bucket, I have plain tap water.' The professor continued with her lecture, but that only made Cat more irritated.

'In the red bucket, I have a liquid that looks, smells and even tastes like water. But if it came in contact with certain materials like cotton or wool, it would become highly volatile causing an explosion.' The professor paused long enough for the words *volatile* and *explosion* to give Cat an idea. As her sister continued with the lecture, the idea became clear. She knew what she had to do.

'What the red bucket contains is, in fact, a brand-new fuel made from recycled organic compounds.' The professor delved deeper into the science, and Cat delved deeper into her idea.

'This revolutionary fuel is incredibly cheap and easy to produce in what is known as a Carbon-free Organic Bio Botanical Liquid Energy Recycling System and is called Redistilled Synthetic Organic Liquid Energy.'

Motes of chalk dust hung suspended in the hard spotlight beam as Yolanda clicked away on the blackboard. As the acronyms took shape, titters and snorts of laughter could be heard throughout the crowd, but the professor didn't seem to notice.

'I need a volunteer to help me demonstrate how this new fuel works,' said the professor.

As hands shot eagerly into the air, Cat flicked open the lid of her pink Zippo and spun the wheel that sparked the flint. The dancing orange flame found the gap in the ugly kid's seat and rapidly charred the tight grey material around the left cheek. Cat had lit the blue touch-paper and now sat back to enjoy the fireworks.

The ugly kid's scream was so loud, it made Cat jump, but it was worth it. The kid leapt out of his chair, hands slapping at the flames eating into his buttocks.

Cat grinned so wide, it almost hurt. The kid had tripped on his own feet and was heading straight for the red bucket.

There was a quiet *splot* as the kid's head, bang on target, disappeared up to the neck. Cat looked up to see her sister's eyes go wide. What was it she'd said about this new fuel and cotton?

The kid stood up, bucket wedged firmly in place, looking like a mutated Wizard of Oz tin man.

There was a moment's silence before a deep bubbling rumble, like a huge boiling kettle, was followed by a muffled explosion.

The bucket expanded suddenly and rocketed across the stage. It glanced off the blackboard, pinged off a roof beam and landed by the rear exit with a clatter.

Cheers and applause erupted from the audience as the kid swayed gently to and fro, smoke drifting from where his school cap and dodgy hairpiece used to be.

Wow thought Cat. *That was impressive.*

'Can I, err...' The professor scratched her chin before continuing. 'Can I have a big cheer for our willing volunteer.'

Whoops and whistles echoed around the walls as the kid staggered, still smoking, back to his seat.

Bugger thought Cat. *The bloody kid's still in the way.*

CHAPTER 6

The Professor

The professor checked her cravat one last time in the mirror. 'Mmm, yes. Presentation is everything,' she said to her reflection, before turning to exit the office.

She trembled slightly at the prospect of moulding young minds and walked silently down the dimly lit hallway, opened a door marked *Lecture Theatre A. No unauthorised entry* and stepped out onto the darkened stage. This was it. A chance to show the dean and the university committee that not only did she have a brilliant mind, but she could also host a lecture without any major disasters. This was due, in no small part, to her sister being seated safely in the audience out of harm's way.

The spotlight lit up pure, brilliant white, and the professor stepped forwards. 'Good evening boys and girls, and welcome to this year's Cambridge Institute Lecture.'

The applause was instantaneous. She had a good feeling about tonight. Everything was planned down to the second, and her idiot sister wasn't backstage, so what could possibly go wrong?

She cleared her throat and introduced herself before wheeling out two buckets. One red and one green. If this went according to plan, she would create a controlled explosion with nothing more than a strip of cotton and a bucket of what appeared to be water. The liquid in the red bucket was, however, a new type of carbon free fuel she had spent months perfecting. Drop a small wad of cotton wool into the liquid and whoof! A six-foot flame would shoot straight to the rafters. It could revolutionise the world's energy supply and give the kids a really cool firework display, as well. What's not to like?

'Some chemicals look, smell and even feel identical but can behave in radically different ways.' Everything had gone smoothly apart from a few snorts of laughter as she chalked up the acronyms. Redistilled Synthetic Organic Liquid Energy? She didn't get it. Why was that so funny? 'I need a volunteer to help me demonstrate how this new fuel works.'

A few hands shot up, but she was surprised when an odd-looking kid in a tight-fitting school uniform screamed and flew out of his seat. *He's certainly an enthusiastic little chap* thought the professor, as the boy hurtled towards the stage.

There was something wrong. The kid wasn't slowing down. If he kept going at that rate, he'd land, cap first, in the red bucket.

Yolanda's brain did a quick calculation. School caps: Wool, cotton, man-made fibres. She took a step back, and then she took another. This wasn't going to end well.

The quiet *splot* of the kid's oversized head wedging in the bucket galvanised the professor into action. She took another step back and hid behind the blast-screen.

Through the bullet-proof glass window, she watched in horror as the kid staggered to his feet, bucket jammed firmly in place. Her analytical eye scanned the scene. What was wrong with the kid's feet? Was one bigger than the other or was it a trick of the light? And why was his left buttock smoking?

She recognized the deep bubbling rumble. A lethal chemical reaction was taking place that could only mean one thing.

The muffled explosion that followed sounded just like the underground dynamite test she'd carried out to rid the garden of moles.

The bucket expanded violently as if it was made of rubber and shot across the stage towards the blackboard. If it hit the blackboard at forty-five to fifty degrees, it should deflect at an upward trajectory, ricochet off the roof truss and land safely by the rear fire exit. She crossed her claws. She wasn't usually superstitious, but this was a situation that could do with as much help as possible.

A second later, the bucket lay crumpled and smouldering near the back doors, and the acrid smell of vaporised school cap and burnt human hair lay heavy on the air.

There was half a beat of silence from the audience. She hadn't killed someone, had she? That wouldn't look good on her CV. The dean took a dim view of death during a lecture. Cheers and whoops erupted from the crowd. Nobody was dead. That meant she wasn't out of a job. The professor stepped from behind the blast-screen to see the big kid swaying back and forth, blue smoke drifting from his bald head.

'Can I, err...' She scratched her chin. What was she going to say? Time stretched out, and the cheering was dying down. She had to say something before they realised what had just happened. That's when a little voice in the back of her mind spoke up. *Make it look as if you meant it to happen.* She looked up and smiled broadly. 'Can I have a big cheer for our willing volunteer?'

The crowd went wild. She'd got away with it. She quickly looked along the rows of cheering children. Now where was... Just before the kid sat back down, the professor glimpsed a familiar figure. Her sister, Cat, was seated directly behind the kid and was grinning so widely, it looked as though her face would split, and her shoulders were going up and down in silent laughter.

I knew it, thought the professor. *My bloody sister's got something to do with this*

The ugly kid with the discoloured nose smouldered gently in his seat. Wisps of pale-blue smoke rose from a patchy, soot blackened scalp giving the impression of a scale model of a battlefield.

The professor smiled again before addressing the audience once more. 'Thanks again to our brave vict... err, volunteer. Anyway...' It was time to change the subject and steer the kids' minds away from the near disaster and towards a new subject. 'There are three bowls in front of me, and each contains a separate ingredient. Sulphur.' She pointed to the first bowl. 'Saltpetre.' She pointed to the second bowl. 'And in the third bowl we have carbon. On their own they are perfectly safe, but when mixed together they create an explosive mixture.' She paused for effect before continuing. 'They create gunpowder!'

She pretended to scan the crowd. 'May I have a second volunteer?' Fewer hands shot up this time. Hardly surprising considering what had just happened. There was only one volunteer the professor was really interested in, even though she hadn't even put her paw up. 'You in the Dolly Parton wig. Step up onto the stage and put these safety goggles on.' She knew she was being a bit too snappy, but she had to get the situation under control.

Cat tottered up the stairs on her glittery gold heels, handbag swinging from her elbow.

'You set light to that poor kid's backside,' whispered the professor. 'There's no point denying it, I know it was you. What do you think you're playing at?'

Cat shrugged. 'I don't know what you mean.'

The professor bit down on her temper. She recognised the sheepish grin but wasn't about to let her irresponsible sibling ruin this lecture. 'Hold this,' she hissed and thrust a lit taper into Cat's paw. 'And don't do a bloody thing until I tell you to.' *It was far better to have the idiot inside the tent pissing out,* thought Yolanda as she turned back to face the audience. 'When I mix these harmless ingredients together, give them a stir and put a lit taper to them, they'll go with a bang.' She nodded to Cat. 'Stand well back and touch the taper to the black powder.'

Cat swung around, handbag arcing towards the bowl. The professor watched in impotent horror as the pale-pink bag hit it, sending it flying into the audience at the exact moment the glowing taper touched down.

A blinding flash flared from the spinning container as it hurtled towards the big ugly kid with the smouldering head. Why then, in the name of prawns, was he smiling? His grinning face vanished in the blast.

The smoke slowly cleared, and the professor looked urgently around the room. Where was the kid?

As if she could read her mind, Cat piped up. 'He's

over there by the door.'

A crumpled pile of arms, legs and splintered chair parts lay ten feet away under a flickering fire exit sign swinging dangerously from one bracket.

'Come on,' said the professor. 'I think we'd better leave.'

Paramedics were busy shovelling the kid onto a stretcher. Cat had probably cost Yolanda her job, but there was no point getting angry as the idiot probably didn't even realise what she'd done. She had to get the maniac out of there whilst all the attention was on the victim, though, and she had a good idea how.

'I've got a nice bottle of vintage port in my office. Let's have a drink and a chat.'

CHAPTER 7

Ralph

R alph had the right to be pleased with himself. After all, he'd successfully laid the trap, avoided any unnecessary violence with the caretaker and got into the lecture without anybody figuring out his true age. Of course he wasn't nine-years-old. What a bunch of mugs.

The only downside, though, was sitting through some dusty old lecture about… what was it again? Explosive chemicals, or something? All he had to do was be patient. As his dad used to tell him all the time; keep your eyes on the prize. Usually whilst he was administering a hearty slippering for whatever happened to be *sin of the day*.

The house-lights dimmed before a spotlight speared the darkness. A small black cat in a billowing velvet cape wafted across the stage and smiled, showing a pair of brilliant white fangs.

Ralph chuckled to himself. Who did the stupid feline think it was, Dracula? He half listened as it chuntered on about carbon-free fuel and buckets. Redistilled Synthetic Organic Liquid Energy, seriously? A tankful of unleaded RSOLE, please. Christ! The fucking animal might be a genius, but it had bugger-all common sense. He leaned back in his chair and shook his head. Was it getting warm in here or was that just his nerves kicking in? A faint smoky scent registered, just as a sharp pain seared his left buttock. He leapt from his seat, an animalistic screech piercing the pain. The sound that registered couldn't be his own scream, could it? Before he had a chance to digest the possibilities, his right foot fought a short battle with his over-sized prosthetic left and lost.

A red bucket. Why was that so important? His arse was on fire. Surely a red bucket was a fire bucket? His synapses sparked and crackled. Didn't the cat-professor say something about cotton and explosions? His cap. His fifty percent cotton, twenty five percent wool and twenty five percent man-made materials cap. The logic circuits in his over-heated brain connected with a painful clunk. He was stumbling towards an explosion, and that explosion was about to involve his own head.

The slopping clear liquid in the bucket really did look like water and the closer he got to it, the more fervently he prayed it was exactly that. Water. His subconscious, however, knew otherwise and had busted through his mental defences. *Water? Yeah, you wish!*

Gravity took hold and pulled him towards the pail of liquid death. Unfortunately, his head had missile-lock and wasn't about to miss. *Splot!* A shiver ran through him as the icy liquid soaked through his cap and mop-head wig. He staggered upright and gripped the bucket in both hands. Damn, it was jammed solid. If it wasn't for the cap and the janitorial hair-piece, it wouldn't have got stuck.

The damned water, or whatever the hell it was, was warming up and was continuing to warm up. In fact it was heading rapidly towards bloody hot. The near-scalding liquid had started a deep bubbling rumble that built steadily in pitch and intensity. The chemical reaction that professor was going on about was happening. It was happening to him! Right now!

A deep boom was followed by a clattering crash, whoops, cheers and wild applause. What the hell just happened?

'Can I have a big cheer for our willing volunteer?' The cat-professor had just called him a willing volunteer. Willing? His buttocks had just spontaneously combusted, and his head had been damned-near blown off his shoulders. Only a hardcore masochist would volunteer for a stunt like that.

He felt for his cap but found nothing but a hairless scalp. The fucking animal had blown his toupee up! It was only a replacement mop-head with a haircut, but that wasn't the point. It had got him this far without anyone noticing that he wasn't a kid. Without it he could very well get busted and end up in jail.

He stumbled offstage and headed towards his seat. Pulling up short, he stared, rubbed his eyes, then stared some more. A bright yellow raincoat, a three-foot-high Dolly Parton wig and tabby fur. The sodding midas cat! And it was grinning at him! It's funny how small details jump out during moments of stress. It was holding a bright pink lighter.

The pieces slotted into place. The bastard cat had set light to his arse for some unknown reason and was now gloating about it.

Ralph's brain re-evaluated the situation. Eyes on the prize? It was right there. There was no need to kidnap the professor now. Only, if he did, he could pick up a nice fat ransom from the university and catch the midas cat. Win, win. What's not to like?

He took his seat once again and nodded to himself. He liked his new plan. Yes. He liked it a lot.

Thoughts of riches and, God yes, a leg over pushed the pain and embarrassment to the back of his mind.

'May I have a second volunteer?' The prof was looking for another victim. Well, this time it wasn't going to be him. He edged forwards on his seat. Psycho-kitty wasn't nuking his bum a second time.

'You in the Dolly Parton wig. Step up onto the stage and put these safety goggles on.'

The professor was calling up her sister. Ralph grinned. Seeing the midas cat blown off stage by dangerous chemicals would be something worth seeing.

'When I mix these harmless ingredients together, give them a stir and put a lit taper to them, they'll go with a bang,' said the professor.

Yeah, and it'll serve the bloody midas cat right, thought Ralph and grinned even wider.

'Stand back and touch the taper to the black powder.' The professor covered her eyes with a pair of over-sized goggles. The midas cat's handbag swung in a graceful arc towards the bowl of black powder and clipped the edge, sending it spinning just as the taper's glowing tip touched down.

Ralph's grin froze as a blinding flash wiped out his vision. Then everything went black.

CHAPTER 8

The Cat

A pleasant tingly sensation ruffled Cat's fur as the ugly kid got a second blasting. *Serves the fat-headed git right*, thought Cat. *Blocking my view. What does he expect, sympathy?*

'Come on,' said Yolanda. 'I think we'd better leave.'

Cat held back for a second longer. Paramedics using shovels to scoop up explosion victims wasn't an everyday occurrence.

A black paw alighted gently on Cat's shoulder. 'I've got a nice bottle of vintage port in my office.' That got Cat's attention. She turned towards the side exit.

'Let's have a drink and a chat.' Yolanda held the door, and Cat stepped through into a dimly lit corridor that smelled faintly of gunpowder residue.

Cat had always loved her sister's office. It was

full of fascinating stuff, like the tiny robots that turned the pages of the book you were reading whilst you ate a prawn cocktail sandwich.

She breathed deeply as antique books and old leather underscored by the faint perfume of furniture polish filled her senses. Another thing Cat liked was the professor's private drinks cabinet. None of your supermarket muck, oh no. This was the good stuff. Upwards of a grand a bottle for the collectable single malt and as for the vintage port, Yolanda was rumoured to own the finest collection in Britain. Expensive, tastes nice and gets you pissed. Sorted!

'Mmm, looks like the janitor has done what I asked and left a bowl of prawns out for supper.' Yolanda's eyes had widened to huge glowing green orbs. Cat knew how much her sister loved seafood.

'If we're going to do this,' said Cat, 'we'd better do it properly.' She opened the drinks cabinet and pulled out a bottle and two glasses. 'I'll pour the drinks and you find some bread and thousand-island sauce.'

'Ah.' Yolanda nodded. 'I like your thinking. Prawn cocktail sandwiches.' She turned the door handle. 'I'll be back in a whisker's twitch.'

Two sizeable doorsteps oozed tangy orange sauce onto the walnut desk.

'Nicely done,' said Cat.

'Yes, I thought so.' Yolanda's white claws extended as she reached a paw for the plate.

'A drink first, though.' Cat held out a cut crystal goblet.

'Oh yes.' The professor's paw hovered over the sandwiches before withdrawing to take hold of the proffered drink. She tilted the desktop lamp and held the glass up to the light. '1964. A good year, I think you'll find.'

Cat didn't bother looking at her port. What was the point? The point was teeth, gums, stomach, pissed. She stared at the ceiling through the bottom of the empty glass. 'Any chance of another?'

Yolanda shook her head and tutted.

Why her sister got all precious about her booze collection was beyond Cat. Yes, it tasted good and got you wasted, but so did home-brewed scrumpy. Cat sunk her second drink and burped. 'Let's eat.'

'In a minute,' said Yolanda. 'Grab the sarnies and follow me. I think the weather's cleared up.'

'So?'

'I want to show you something.' Yolanda exited through the door on the left marked *roof.*

The breeze had a sharp edge to it which, luckily for Cat, was somewhat blunted by the two large ports. 'What are we doing up here?' Cat lit up a cheroot and screwed it into her *Lady Penelope* cigarette holder.

'Up there.' Yolanda pointed almost straight up.

'Up where?' What the hell her sister was pointing at and why she'd dragged her up here onto the battlements, only God knew, because she sure as hell didn't.

'If you look to the right of Saturn, you'll be able to make out that new comet I discovered.'

'Where?' To the right of Saturn? She might just as well as said *to the right of Beijing town centre car park*. She twirled around to look up at the night sky, cigarette swinging in a wide arc.

A sizzling hiss was followed by liquid screaming as the thrashing shape of a man burst from the shadows, tripped on a low wall and fell howling over the battlements. It looked to Cat as if someone was learning to fly without a plane.

The jerking body hit the gravel path with a muffled thud and went still.

Yolanda peered down at the walkway. 'Who *was* that?'

Cat shrugged. 'I haven't the foggiest. More importantly, though. Where are the sandwiches?'

CHAPTER 9

The Professor

The evening air had a frost-laden snap to it, making Yolanda shiver in spite of her thick fur and velvet cloak. The roof was a great place to empty your head of the everyday detritus of life in order to create some breathing space for serious scientific thinking. It was at this very spot that she'd made the discovery whilst meditating on the quantum dynamics of chaos theory.

'Up there.' She pointed a paw towards the sky. At the edge of naked visibility was the comet she'd stumbled upon purely by chance.

'Up where?'

Getting her sister engaged in an intellectual discussion could be more challenging than the science itself. 'If you look to the right of Saturn, you'll be able to just make out that new comet I discovered.'

'Where?'

The idiot had been looking everywhere but in the right direction, when she suddenly spun around. Yolanda leaped backwards just in time as Cat whirled unsteadily on her heels, wig canting dangerously to starboard.

At that exact moment, a person-shaped shadow slid out from behind the college spire. A man was on the roof and was creeping towards the plate of sandwiches. Why on earth had somebody followed them all the way up here just to steal their supper?

Yolanda stared in amazement as the burglar and her sister's glowing cigarette reached the same point at the same time. Chaos theory in action! What were the chances?

A rock-splintering scream sliced through the cold night air and the thief tumbled over the parapet, arms thrashing wildly. A muffled thud silenced the agonised cries. The supper-snatcher was obviously unconscious but more likely dead, given the height of the building and terminal velocity. She peered over the edge. 'Who *was* that?'

Cat shrugged. 'I haven't got the foggiest. More importantly, though. Where are the sandwiches?' Yolanda leaned over the battlements and studied the crumpled heap at the base of the wall. Next to the unmoving body lay a smear of prawn cocktail sauce and the scattered remains of two large doorsteps. 'Down there.'

'Oh bugger,' said Cat.

CHAPTER 10

Ralph

Voices drifted on Ralph's consciousness. It was like trying to listen to a slightly out-of-tune radio.

'He's stable... No broken... Miracle...'

A sudden jolt pulled him rudely from his semi-coma. He sat up as his memory jump started. The lecture. The midas cat. The explosion. 'Where the hell am I?' His voice, cracked and raspy, sounded alien to him.

'You're in the ambulance.' A soothing female voice came from behind the dazzling white light that flashed from one eye to the other and back again. 'Sorry about the bumpy ride. It's the speed humps.'

He was in an ambulance. He was safe. He was on his way to hospital. His brain turned the information over slowly. The hospital was not the university. His ticket back into Lauren's life was back there *at* the university, and *he* was moving steadily away from it. 'Got to...' He didn't get the chance to finish the sentence. Spending God knows how long in a hospital bed wasn't going to win his wife back. The steady beeping of the heart monitor accelerated rapidly before cutting to a solid tone as Ralph tore off the sticky patches. Before he had a chance to over-think it, he flung open the ambulance doors and stepped off into space.

The paramedic's yells quickly faded as he hit the tarmac. The world spun as he bounced off the rain slicked surface and slammed into a bollard. His head swam as he pulled himself upright. What had they given him in the ambulance? Whatever it was, it was good shit! He couldn't feel a thing. If his head was hanging by a thread, he was bloody sure he wouldn't notice. He looked around, trying to get his bearings. 'Oh bollocks!' The ambulance was doing a u turn. If he didn't get out of sight, they'd take him back to hospital, and his one chance of happiness would evaporate in a wail of sirens.

'Hey, everybody!' Cheering and applause echoed around Ralph's head. 'Welcome back to Hide or Die!'

'Fuck off and leave me alone!' That's all he needed. Hallucinogenic game-show hosts buggering up his chances of happiness.

'Will Ralph escape the ambulance, or will the paramedics call the police? Tune in after the adverts to find out.'

Oh, great. It's always the bloody adverts. A cheesy jingle from the seventies played in full Dolby surround sound. Even worse, it was a cat food commercial.

The drugs the paramedics had given him must have reacted with the painkillers already sloshing about in his system. Because this time, he could actually see the damned screen. Mister Smarmy-Game-show-Host was wearing a pink and green spotted bow tie over a purple shirt. That was enough to put anyone off their stride.

'We've got a brand-new show coming later.' The trippy screen flickered and bounced as Ralph took off with a limping run down the nearest side street.

'It'll be a fight to the death in the pilot episode of...' The deepening shadows did nothing to diminish the bright neon glare of... 'One Man and his Cat!' A cartoon feline wearing an enormous pink wig cartwheeled through Ralph's eyeline.

The self-administered slap was hard enough to light up a stinging burn and send white spots of light dancing across the drug-induced TV screen.

The picture turned to snowy static for an instant but returned a second later. How the hell was he going to function with this guff going on in his head? He hauled back and landed a whip-crack right hander blacking out the trip-o-vision. Good, he hadn't gone totally mad. At least, not yet, anyway. He had to get out of sight, though, because the strobing blue pulsing from the end of the road definitely wasn't a travelling night club.

He ducked into a tiny front garden with a perfectly square privet hedge. Peering out through the neatly clipped foliage gave him a not-entirely clear view of the street beyond, but at least he could see the flashing blue lights fading into the rapidly cooling night.

Now all he had to do was get back to the university and collect two comatose cats.

'Oi!' The shout came from behind him. He leaped to his feet and spun to face the voice.

'What the fuck are you doing in my front garden, you little creep?'

The light from the open doorway backlit a monster that very nearly filled it entirely.

'Maureen, get some clothes on! It's that fucking peeping tom again. He ain't getting away this time, though.'

Light spilled out around the monster as he stepped onto the front path. 'Oh, Jesus! It's a mutant!' The monster home-owner stopped short, fists raised.

This was it. His only chance. Ralph's burns and prosthetic nose had saved his life. At least they would if he could get his legs to obey him.

'Get here, you little goblin!'

A meaty fist grabbed a handful of blazer sleeve tearing it at the shoulder, nearly spinning Ralph around as he crashed through the garden gate and hop-limped towards the main road.

'That's it!' yelled Mister Maureen. 'Run, you little perv.'

The lecture theatre was in darkness. 'Show must be over,' muttered Ralph as he headed for the side exit. A sulphurous after-burn stung the back of his throat as he stepped through into the wood-panelled corridor. What quantity of explosives had the damned cat used if he could still smell it? He was bloody lucky not to have been killed.

He stepped as quietly as he could. His heart pounded so hard, he could almost feel the swish of blood in his veins, and his head throbbed in rhythm with his pulse. Not long now. If he could keep the hallucinations at bay for just a little longer, he couldn't fail.

A muted greenish glow spilled from a gap at the door's edge. It was slightly ajar. He had to be extra careful, then. He wiped his sweat-sticky palms on his school shorts and slid forwards, mindful of his oversized artificial foot.

He held his breath and strained for the slightest sound. No talking, no movement. Just the unwavering marking of time by the antique clock.

Well, this was it. He was going in. He eased the door open expecting to find two unconscious cats.

Nothing. Where the hell were they? The drugged prawns had gone, and if he'd got the dosage right, the cats should have succumbed pretty much instantly. No, this wasn't right. He stared around the room hoping for inspiration.

'We're at a critical part of the show, folks,' said Mister Smarmy-Gameshow.

'Oh, just leave me the fuck alone, will you?'

'Wouldn't you like a clue?'

Ralph nodded. What the hell was he doing? He was accepting clues from somebody that didn't exist.

Ralph's pretend friend burst into a tuneless rendition of an old Drifters' song, *up on the roof.*

Fuck me, thought Ralph. *It keeps getting better. The tosser's singing now.* No. Wait. That *was* the clue. Up on the roof. The bloody cats are up on the sodding roof.

He jammed the water pistol into the waistband of his shorts and gently opened the door. If they were up there, that meant they were still conscious, and if they were conscious, that meant they hadn't eaten the prawns. He'd have to inject the cats directly instead.

He reached into his inside blazer pocket where the hypo sat, snuggled amongst the tissues. There had to be nearly half of it left. He rummaged about. It had to be in there somewhere. He was sure he hadn't dropped it. 'Shit!' Grabbing the business end was not a good idea. That needle strike would cost him if any of the trank got into his system.

He took a step and grasped the door handle as the office pitched violently. The muted glow of the desk lamp had increased in intensity, throwing grotesque shadows around the walls. His stomach lurched as the room rode up the face of a non-existent wave.

Oh God, no. He hadn't got away with it. Ketamine plus a near overdose of painkillers, plus whatever the paramedics had pumped into him were about to join forces in his bloodstream. They were launching a frontal attack on his brain. Any minute now he was either going to pass out or go on a mother of a bad trip, so he had to find those damned felines and secure them somehow before finding a nook to ride out the effects of the drugs.

He stepped onto the risers leading to the roof and squinted as he hit the open air. The icy breeze sliced into the sheen of sweat, tingling Ralph's forehead. Everything felt amplified and wrong. He could smell the cold and feel the pricks of starlight, but ahead of him, standing by the low castellated wall, were his tickets to wealth and happiness. There they were. All he had to do was catch them and all his problems would go away.

He blinked away a sting of sweat, opened his eyes, then closed them again. No. It couldn't be. Sitting on a raised battlement and grinning an overly wide smile of undiluted insincerity was Mister Smarmy-Gameshow. Not a voice in his head or on a hallucinatory telly, but a real-life, flesh and blood bastard. He winked at Ralph and pointed.

Ralph followed where the finger pointed. On a low wall were two doorstep sandwiches. He looked up at Mister Smarmy-Gameshow who smiled even wider and nodded. It was another clue. He had to get to the sandwiches and what? Force feed the two furry idiots? Why? Wait a minute! Prawn cocktail, missing prawns and both cats wide awake and un-ketamined. They'd made sandwiches out of the trap he'd laid and forgotten to eat them.

Mister Smarmy-Gameshow gave a thumbs-up before putting a finger to his lips. Yes, yes. He knew. Stealth but to what end? How could he force the food into their mouths? One, maybe, but the other one would escape and call the police.

Mister Smarmy-Gameshow gave a pantomime sigh before making the shape of a gun with his hand and pointing it at the cats.

Clarity is a wonderful thing. Especially in the middle of a conversation with an imaginary TV presenter. He was armed. Of course he was. The thing pushing into his left testicle was only a cheap kids' toy, but to a cat it may just as well have been loaded with tank-busting shells. A persuasion device of the utmost quality. A bloody water-pistol!

He slid out from the covering shadow of the gothic spire and eased his way towards the sandwiches, right hand gripping the pistol lodging against his scrotum. He snatched up the plate and pulled on the pistol, but it did a *sword in the stone* and stuck fast. Bugger it!

A sudden movement pulled his vision away from the food. What was the stupid midas cat doing now?

It was spinning around on its ridiculously high heels, its Dolly Parton wig sliding sideways off its head. Priceless! Damn, that was funny! His grin froze into a grimace as the flaring cherry of the midas cat's cigarette sizzled his right eye.

An unearthly wail split the atoms of oxygen around him, causing the air to ripple. The realisation that it was his own screaming registered just as his left foot twisted sideways and caught on the low part of the wall.

Time slowed, and he watched in detached fascination as the spinning sandwiches separated before splattering on the gravel path.

Then everything went black.

THE MIDAS CAT
- PART THREE.

Man Friday the Thirteenth.

CHAPTER 1

Ralph

The ketamined prawn-cocktail sandwich incident was now a distant memory, and Ralph felt fit and well; physically, anyway. Standing in the concourse of Heathrow Airport, he looked at his reflection in W H Smith's window. A perfect smile looked back. Topped by an exquisitely carved aquiline nose and a thick, wavy thatch of hair, the past two years felt like a horror movie starring somebody else. There is no midas cat. It had taken him two years of therapy to be able to say that. Uncle Ranulph hadn't exactly hindered matters, either. He hadn't hindered to the tune of three million.

It didn't bother Ralph that he had inherited a small fortune because of a gross typing error. He knew damned well that his cousin Rolph was the rightful heir, but after all the shit he'd been through, he thought he deserved a break. Besides, nobody dare get too close as he sat in the solicitor's office, what with the fleas and ticks pinging off his leprous donkey jacket.

He'd flashed a toothless, scabby grin at that tosser Rolph when the will had been read. Oh, happy memories. He took one last look at his re-constructed face in the shop window, and his brow fought against the Botox as he tried to frown. Reflected directly behind him was something his therapist had convinced him didn't exist.

Ducking out of sight between Subway and the Ann Summer's shop were a pair of pointed ears and a long, slender tabby tail.

His head shot round. Holiday makers, businessmen, excited children and nothing else. His pulse had picked up the pace and was galloping down the home straight. 'There is no midas cat. There is *no* midas cat!' He drove home the last *no* with the fervour of a preacher having witnessed a miracle. The mantra had worked wonders and he was now clean and midas cat-free. Right now, though, its power seemed to be slipping. The midas cat couldn't be real, though, could it? His sanity depended on its non-existence.

Curiosity rose in Ralph like the acid bile he had to swallow. He wiped his sweat-slicked palms on his chinos and forced his legs to move.

Around the corner was either his own turbocharged imagination, or God's vengeance for keeping his mouth shut during the reading of the will. 'There is no midas cat, there is no midas cat,' he muttered as he forced himself around the corner onto the main concourse.

'There is no... What the fuck?' Stripy fur, whiskers and long tails were everywhere. Midas cats by the dozen had invaded the airport, and nobody had raised the alarm.

'Oi, don't just stand there blocking my doorway!' The painted smile on the clown's face did nothing to hide his annoyance. 'You going in, or not? If you are, that'll be two quid.'

A large banner stretched across the front of the shop. It read; *Kidsave Children's Charity Annual Fundraiser. Dress as a cat day.*

'Oh, no. Sorry.' Ralph sidestepped the clown only to get squirted by the idiot's joke flower for his troubles.

Children were lining up to buy cat onesies and to have their faces made up. Not midas cats. Children dressed as cats. One child, however, stuck out of the crowd. It had the biggest, greenest, glassiest eyes. The bloody kid had midas cat eyes and stared unblinkingly at him from over the top of a huge cloud of candyfloss. Ralph felt sick. Puking over Bobo wasn't an option, though. He slumped against the litter bin, pulling in huge lungfuls of air. He needed a drink. His therapist had told him to keep away from alcohol. A small scotch to calm his nerves, though. Extenuating circumstances and all that. If this wasn't bloody extenuating, he didn't know what was.

Now where was the damned bar? He passed a duty-free shop. It was the same one he'd passed a couple of minutes earlier. He was going around in circles, so he stopped to get his bearings. 'Err. Phones R Us on the right. That means I have to turn, erm…' A flash of patterned fur registered in his peripheral vision. One of those sodding kids was at the till in the duty-free shop. This was getting a bit much. He had to find the bar, and soon, if he had any chance of soothing his battered nerves. 'There is no midas cat, there is no midas cat. It's only a kid in a onesie.' He took one last look to re-assure himself. Kids don't buy single malt scotch, though.

He looked away. No, he mustn't let his over-heated imagination rule his life. There was no way that customer was the midas cat. 'There is no midas cat,' he murmured. A bead of cold sweat popped on his forehead and tracked an itchy path down his nose. He ignored it, shook his head and looked again.

The hard white of the fluorescent tubes lit up an empty shop. Apart from a bored looking girl on the till, there was nobody in the duty-free, only a faint sound of music drifting from around the corner. He could just make out the lyrics to *Stand and Deliver*. 'There is *no* midas cat, God dammit!'

His therapist was right. He did need this holiday. He needed to get away from it all, and *The Rob-*

inson Crusoe Experience on his very own deserted Caribbean island was about as far away from it as he could possibly get. Just him, his own Man Friday, beach barbeques, snorkelling, swimming, and nobody else for miles.

He'd arrived at the bar with no memory of how he got there, and it looked as if all the passengers in the airport had decided to join him.

'Excuse me... Sorry... Pardon me.' He jostled to the front and waved a twenty at the barman. 'Single, no, make it a double scotch. No ice. Cheers, mate.'

The fat clown from the Kidsave charity plonked himself down on the barstool to Ralph's right. Ralph shuddered. There was something about clowns that made him want to punch them. He took his scotch and change and swung around to his left before Bobo, or whatever his name was, engaged him in conversation. His gaze drifted until it locked onto the kid. It must have come from that charity event because it was still in its onesie and face paint. Seated at the far end of the curved bar, it looked at him from over the top of the foam on its pint of bitter. They let kids into airport bars now, do they? No. That wasn't right. He stared harder and realisation slammed into him. 8-year-olds don't drink real ale. The glassy green eyes staring unblinkingly back at him didn't belong to any kid, though.

He recited the mantra, necking his drink in one. 'Same again, please!' he shouted to the barman.

'Steady on there,' said Bobo, 'it's not a race.'

Ralph fought the urge to bury his fist into the middle of that stupid red nose, snatched up his drink and sunk it. He slammed the empty glass on the bar, closed his eyes and started counting aloud. 'One, two, three...' He reached twenty and opened them again. The midas cat had vanished. That's if it was ever there in the first place. He held a quivering hand in front of his face.

'I hope that's not the hand you shoot with,' quipped bobo.

'Oh, piss off, you creepy bastard!' Ralph shoved his way out of the bar towards the departure lounge. 'There is no midas cat, there is no midas cat!'

CHAPTER 2

The Cat

C at fished in her onesie. 'I know I had it earlier.' It wasn't as if the check-in queue hadn't taken long enough already. Cat glanced back at the red-faced man who was next in line. He made a show of checking his watch and then glaring hard at Cat.

It wasn't her fault that the tabby onesie had too many pockets. How was she to know which pocket she'd put the ticket in? She was pissed when she put it in there. 'Got it!'

'Thank fuck for that,' murmured Mister Red-face.

'Oh no, sorry. Tesco Clubcard voucher.' Cat grinned in what she hoped was an apologetic manner as Mister Red-face muttered obscenities from behind her.

'No, wait. Here it is.' Cat produced her airline

ticket with a flourish.

'Bloody well better be.' Mister Red-face shuffled up behind Cat, nudging her forwards. 'Sodding kid. Where are its parents, that's what I'd like to know?'

The far side of check-in meant duty-free booze and fags and Cat wasted no time before heading straight for the shops.

'Wow!' A girl of about seven dressed in an identical cat onesie, her face an artwork of feline stripes and whiskers, caught hold of Cat's arm. 'Your cat make-up is brilliant!' She grinned, showing a gap-toothed smile. 'It almost looks real. Best one I've seen today.'

Cat tilted her head. What was the small human prattling on about? Cat decided to humour the miniature person and smiled back.

'And the teeth!' The girl's eyes bugged in her head. 'Mummy!' She tugged hard on what must have been her mother's sleeve. At least Cat hoped it was her mother and not some random stranger.

'I want some cat teeth. Can I have cat teeth, pleeease?

The attention of the small monkey descendant was momentarily elsewhere, so Cat used the hiatus to quietly slip away.

Sliding between shoppers, Cat reached W H Smiths before pausing briefly to get her bearings. 'Let me see now. Subway? No. Ann Summers? I think not. Ooh, what's down there?' Cat slid between the two shops onto the main concourse and came to a sudden and complete stop. Miniature humans were everywhere, and all of them were dressed just like the little girl from earlier. All of them were dressed as Cat! Pointy ears, furry tails, whiskers and stripy faces bounded and bounced around outside of a large glass-fronted shop. A banner with the words; *Kidsave Children's Charity Annual Fundraiser. Dress as a cat day* was draped across the outside of the shop. Cat grinned. How cool was that? She sauntered past the fat clown with the pink fright wig and wandered into the shop. Free candy floss. Yes! Cat knew it would give her a sugar-rush, making her a bit hyper, but who cares? It was free.

'Oi, don't just stand there blocking my doorway!' The clown was having a go at some gormless twonk who'd decided that a busy doorway was a great place to stop. This might lead to a fight. Cat stared at the two men over the top of her candy floss. She'd never seen a clown in a fight before. This could be interesting.

The clown scowled, which was really odd, what with the huge painted grin and over-the-top eyebrows.

'You going in, or not? If you are, that'll be two quid.'
The gormless twonk with the Liberace hair seemed to come to his senses. 'Oh, no. Sorry.' He sidestepped to let the clown into the shop and got suckered by his squirty flower. Well, that served

the plank right, but Cat was nonetheless disappointed by the lack of clown violence.

Mister Gormless had wandered off, no doubt to block some other shop doorway. Realising there was to be no squeaky nosed bare-knuckle match, Cat left the shop. It was time to get her booze and fags, anyway.

Opposite Phones R Us was a vast open-fronted store full of alcohol of all kinds and many types of tobacco products. *Here we go* thought Cat as she plunged into the cigarette aisle. 'French fags, eh?' Cat turned the box of two hundred cancer sticks over in her paws. 'Well, I am off to foreign parts,' she said to the empty store. 'They speak French in the Caribbean…I think.' Cat wasn't sure and didn't really care as a bottle of single malt was calling her from a neighbouring aisle.

The check-out girl looked beyond bored and well on her way to a tedium-induced coma, but what caught Cat's attention was the gormless twonk from the charity event. He was outside the shop looking around aimlessly. Cat handed the girl the bottle of scotch but didn't take her eyes from the dopey git outside. There was something strangely familiar about him. Try as she might, though, she couldn't place him. She shrugged. What did it matter, anyway? She had a box of eau de merde fags, and a quart of single malt heaven.

As Cat left the shop, she couldn't help noticing Mister Gormless. He stood with his eyes shut, swaying ever so slightly back and forth. He was also talking to himself. In an airport full of armed police? Seriously? Cat stuffed in her ear buds and skipped off to the airport bar. Stand and Deliver, one of Cat's favourite songs, blasted from her iPod as she flowed around the tightly packed people and ordered her first drink of the day.

'Mmm, beer.' Cat's paw closed around the cool curve of the glass, condensation damping her pad. She lifted the pint of foaming ale to her lips and stopped. Over the froth, she could see the gormless twonk at the far end of the curved bar staring straight at her, and he looked terrified. Then Cat saw the fat clown from the Kidsave charity. No wonder he was terrified. The Malodorous Beast from The Big Top was sitting right next to him.

Mister Gormless had downed two large scotches in quick succession and had closed his eyes. He was counting aloud to nobody in particular. Dopey prat. Cat sunk her pint and headed off to the departure lounge before the prat had reached five.

The woman seated on Cat's left smiled, her lone tooth standing sentinel over the foothills of her chins. 'George.' Her southern American drawl reminded Cat of the classic movie *Gone with the Wind.* Either that or *The Texas Chainsaw Massacre.*

The man on Cat's right spilled over the armrests, his blubber jiggling as he tried to settle into the aeroplane seat. 'Why don't they make seats for normal-sized people, instead of these here kiddy seats?'

'George!' the smile on the woman's face dropped into a well-practised scowl. 'Will you quit fidgeting and listen to me for once in your sorry-ass life?'

George instantly obeyed, his under-sized eyes peering out from the folds of maroon flab. 'Sorry, Cutesy-Pie.'

Cutesy-Pie? They had to have packed the plane especially to re-balance the ballast just because of her!

'Have some consideration for the child, George!' Cutesy-Pie put a bingo-winged arm around Cat's shoulder and gave her a surprisingly gentle squeeze. 'Couldn't you get a seat next to your parents?' Cutesy-Pie wiped away a string of drool with her free hand. 'Don't worry, sweetie. We'll take care of you. Anything you need, you just ask.' Cutesy-Pie leaned across Cat and prodded George, her finger sinking into the roll of belly-jelly. 'George. Won't you look at the child's face painting. It's so good, it could almost be a real cat.'

George nodded. 'Yes, dear.'

'Oh, darling,' said Cutesy-Pie. 'We're takin' off now. Put your seatbelt on.'

It was nice being pampered, but there *was* a limit. Cat clicked her seatbelt shut and stuffed in her ear buds, cranking the volume to drown out Cutesy-Pie. Adam Ant's *Stand and Deliver* blew through Cat's ear hairs just as the sugar rush from the candy floss mingled with the beer in her system. As the plane surged forwards, she threw some moves, the seat in front providing a perfect kick-drum for her back paws.

She was just getting into the zone, when Adam and the Ants cut out without warning. 'Oh bugger.' Her iPod clattered to the floor, pulling out the earphone plug.

'Ahh.' Cutesy-Pie was on her in a flash. 'Have you lost your music machine thingy?'

Yes, thought Cat, *and if you keep your fat arse where it is, I might be able to retrieve it.* There it was, wedged against the floor bracket. She stretched a paw forward. Nearly, nearly. Gotcha!

'Fucking kid's kicking my seat!'
Cat sat up. There was a fight. Having missed out on the clown fight earlier, passenger fighting might make up for it. The only problem was George. He'd stood up and spread out. She couldn't see a thing around his airship of a backside.

'Kill him, George!' Cutesy-Pie had gone a funny shade of pinkie-purple with bright red spots high up on her slab-like cheeks. 'Oh, beautiful child. You don't want to see this. It ain't pretty.' She turned to Cat and shoved a huge round lolly into her lap. 'Here, darlin', you have my lollypop to take your mind off of all this unnecessary violence.'

Cat held up the swirly green, blue and white lolly. It was enormous. It was so big that Cat could barely see over the top.

'Rip the limey's head off!' Cutesy-Pie was really

feeling it. 'He shouldn't pick on small children like that!'

God, this was good. Get in there, George. Cat watched the action from over the top of her lolly. Now George had repositioned himself, Cat could see the opponent.

The gormless twonk from the Kidsave charity event was squaring up to George who, now he'd pulled himself up to his full height, must have topped out at six feet six. This wasn't, to paraphrase Cutesy-Pie, going to be pretty. Cat gripped her lolly stick in anticipation. Seconds away, round one. *Go on, George,* thought Cat. *Get in there, my son!*

'Your bastard kid hasn't stopped kicking me in the back since we took off!' The gormless twonk pointed a finger straight at Cat, opened his mouth and froze. The high colour of anger drained from the top down. He looked as though he was about to faint and spoke a phrase that was barely audible over the plane's engines. 'There is no midas cat, there is no midas cat,' before collapsing into his seat.

'Ah think that just about settles things.' George heaved his massive frame around to face Cat. 'He won't be bothering you no more, child.'
Cat nodded, stuffed her ear buds back in and continued with her seat dancing.

CHAPTER 3

Ralph

The old lady snoozing in the window seat wasn't going to cause any trouble, but unfortunately Ralph didn't think he could say the same for the fat bastards directly behind him. Whilst loading his hand luggage into the overhead locker, he took a peripheral peek. Oh, God they were big. *He* had a face the colour of an over-ripe aubergine and had to have been greased to have fitted in the airline seat. *She* was wearing lipstick a shade above stop-sign red. It clashed horribly with the tight curls of bright ginger hair. If you've got ginger hair, don't wear salmon pink curlers. He was sure there was a law about that somewhere. If there wasn't, there bloody well should be.

He almost didn't notice the kid in the cat onesie squeezed in between Jabba and Mrs The Hut. Must have been to the charity fund raiser at the airport.

Ralph found himself feeling sorry for the poor kid. Having parents like that can't be easy.

'George!'

It keeps getting better, thought Ralph, as the obese woman piped up. They're not only fat, they're sodding hillbillies as well.

Not wanting to make eye contact in case they were hungry, Ralph planted his backside and hunkered down with the airline magazine.

The roar of the plane's engines was perfect for drowning out the Deliverance couple.

The seatbelt sign flashed on. Great. Another step closer to a therapeutic fortnight of tropical peace and quiet. Ralph's eyes closed, and he pictured a turquoise sea washing a platinum beach, hammock strung between two palm trees. Bliss.

The plane broke through the roof of the heavy grey clouds and sunlight flooded the cabin. Thump! That's when the kicking began. Thump, thump! The vision of Caribbean perfection dissolved in an instant. Thump, thump, thump! Any sympathy Ralph may have felt for the hillbilly's kid evaporated. Thump! And what's more, the kid's iPod must have been deafening. Thump! A vaguely familiar rhythm underpinned lyrics that made Ralph reach for the vomit bag. Adam and the Ants? No fucking way! 'There is no midas cat,' he whispered and hoped to hell he was right. Thump! Sodding hillbillies. He'd had enough of their shit! 'Excuse me!' He was a little too snappy with the small be-spectacled man in the aisle seat, but he had a fat father and onesied kid to have a go at.

Ralph clenched his fists, mainly to stop his hands from shaking, as he glared down at the sweaty lard mountain. 'Fucking kid's kicking my seat!' The kid rummaged about under the drop-down tray. Hopefully it had lost its phone, or iPod, or whatever the fuck it was using. *Well,* thought Ralph, *if I find it first, the kid ain't getting it back!*

George pushed himself out into the aisle and stood up. Now there were no armrests to act as dams, the lard river burst its banks and flooded the narrow walkway. Oh. My. God! George stooped to look Ralph in the face. A muscle twitched somewhere under the cherry blancmange near George's left eye, sending a faint ripple across the cheek.

'Kill him, George!' Mrs Deliverance sounded positively gleeful, but Ralph couldn't be a hundred percent sure as he couldn't see around George's bulk.

George took a lumbering step forwards and straightened up. It was like watching an overweight grizzly bear in a tight shirt rear up on its hind legs. *I'm gonna die now.* The thought was calm and peaceful. Whilst the woman made cooing baby-talk to the mini hillbilly, Ralph had resigned himself to certain death. *I'm gonna die now. I know I'm gonna die.* His mind was remarkably clear as he watched George bunch up a meaty fist. He was going to die and the oddest thing about it was the fact that he didn't care.

'Rip the limey's head off!' That snapped him out of his state of resignation. The mono-toothed monstrosity wanted blood. Well, he was damned if any of it was going to be his! He had rights, and he was bloody well going to stand up for them.

'Your bastard kid hasn't stopped kicking me in the back since we took off!' He wasn't going down without a fight. He was in the right and he knew it. He pointed a finger straight at the onesied child, opened his mouth to fire off a barbed insult and froze. A pair of glassy green eyes peered at him from over the top of the biggest lollypop he'd ever seen. The face painting was too realistic. Even though he could only see it from eye-level up, he could have sworn on his sanity that it was the midas cat. The righteous indignant anger gurgled away along with his balance. He gripped the seat in front of him. Confusion filled his head with un-answerable questions. It *was* their kid, wasn't it? If it wasn't, though, then whose was it? His therapist had told him. He'd hammered it into him every week for nearly two years. 'There is no midas cat, there is no midas cat.' The voice was weak and faint and was coming from a long way away, but it was definitely his.

He pushed past the small be-spectacled man without another word.

'Ah think that just about settles things,' said George.

Ralph shut his eyes.

'He won't be bothering you no more, child.' The

plane shook as George poured himself back into his seat.

Thump! Ralph stared numbly at the lap tray as Adam and the Ants drilled into his head.

CHAPTER 4

The Cat

I t had been a fantastic first night. Cat had fallen in with a group of lads from the west coast of Ireland and gone on a pub crawl. It had gone fabulously well until Cat suggested *borrowing* one of the luxury cruisers from the harbour. The lads told Cat she was insane and would have nothing to do with it, but Cat was never one to be put off that easily.

They watched in silence from the top of the harbour wall as twenty million quid's worth of floating opulence burbled out into open water.

Everything went a bit hazy after that. Vague images played in her head about a ship-wreck. Whether she'd run into submerged rocks or not, she wasn't entirely sure, but she remembered the almighty crunch, and the boat sliding gracefully beneath the waves.

How she ended up asleep under the board-walk, God only knows. She stretched and yawned. She needed a hair-of-the-dog and searched her pockets.

The morning sun lit everything with a glaring brightness that lasered into the back of Cat's ret-inas. She squinched her eyes shut and pulled out her hip flask. Hefting it in her paw told her every-thing she needed to know. 'Half full,' she said. 'That'll sort me out.' She popped the lid, tipped her head back and drained the contents in one.

She belched and ambled out onto the white sand. It couldn't have been much more than nine in the morning, but the beach was already buzz-ing. Rows of thatched umbrellas shaded loungers that were draped in towels or scantily clad occu-pants.

She strolled past beachside bars, windsurfer hire, fishing boat charters and finally reached the pedalo man.

Pedaloes weren't luxury yachts, so what could possibly go wrong?

She fished in her pockets. The iPod and portable speakers were luckily untouched by the seawater as were Cat's secret money-pouch and fags that were tucked away deep in her pelt.

The weather report playing from the pedalo man's radio was right and as the sun climbed, so did the temperature. Cat pedalled lazily up and down the beach, a steady squeak coming from the un-oiled craft. The gentle rocking motion of the sea soon conspired with the heat of the day and Cat drifted off into a deep and contented sleep.

Cat opened an eye. The sun was way past its zenith and gradually heading westwards. How long had she been out for? It was only about quarter past ten in the morning when she'd dozed off, and now the day's intense heat had mellowed into a late afternoon warmth.

Cat stretched and looked around. The big hotels, nightclubs and bars had vanished, replaced by a heavily jungled island.

She pedalled ashore and pulled her little boat up beyond the high tide mark. Where the hell was she? 'Only one way to find out.' She strode up the deserted beach and plunged whiskers first into the lush greenery.

She stared about in wonder as she tripped silently through the thick vegetation. She had been walking for five minutes when she stumbled upon something very un-jungle like.

The rust pocked sign was barely visible through the vines and creepers that had smothered it over the years. 'Hello,' said Cat. 'What do we have here?'

She cleared some of the undergrowth. *Property of the US Government. Keep out.* She pulled the remaining greenery from the sign and stepped back, eyes widening in alarm. *Nuclear test site. Trespassers will be shot.*

Cat wondered why the tour operator had failed to mention the weapons testing facility in their brochure. But then again, what *could* they say? Sun, sea and nuclear radiation guaranteed or your money back? She dropped into a crouch, slid under the barbed wire fence and crept forwards. If this place was for real, Cat knew she was in serious trouble for even being on the island in the first place, but she also knew that she *had* to explore. She couldn't help herself. She *was* a cat, after all.

She pulled herself up behind a thick tree trunk and scanned the patches of dappled light up ahead. Shafts of golden late afternoon sun speared the forest's canopy, creating pools of brightness in the damp green shade.

The gun barrel was so well camouflaged, it could almost have been part of the jungle. She stared at the unmoving weapon and eased further down into the thick foliage. Slipping forwards on silent pads, she closed in on the sentry post until it was within a couple of feet.

The long-forgotten machine gun peeped out from under the fat leaves of the tree that had grown out through the middle of the gun-emplacement.

'This place has been abandoned.' The tiny green frog perched on the gun's ammo box blinked up at Cat as if to say *yeah, decades ago.*

Cat straightened up, emboldened by her discovery and plunged ahead.

The iron door hadn't been moved for at least fifty years and had seized open with just enough of a gap for Cat to squeeze through. She ignored the scurrying of rodents and pressed on into the darkness, her eyes quickly adjusting to the dim light.

The electric generator stood block-like in the centre of the room. The sign on the door said: *Service personnel only*. As Cat was the only one here, that made her service personnel. She pressed the starter button. Nothing. Well, what did she expect? Her brother, Jimmy, was handy with his paws and could get most things working. If he was here, what would he do? She walked around the big machine, studying it in detail. That's when she spotted the crank handle. Yep, that's what Jimmy would have done.

After coughing and spluttering for a couple of minutes, the generator settled into a steady rhythm.

Caged bulbs illuminated the bare concrete tunnels of the labyrinthine facility with a pale-yellow light. *Time to explore,* thought Cat and headed up the corridor.

The locker room yielded a pile of mostly useless junk apart from a rusty bicycle, a vintage split-cane fishing rod and reel, and a report on the cannibalistic habits of the native islanders, dated July 1957.

Cannibals only eat humans, thought Cat. No cannibal would ever guess it was Cat, anyway, as she was wearing her onesie. A perfect disguise.

Her belly rumbled. She hadn't eaten since the previous night and needed to catch some dinner.

Rod and reel in paw, she mounted the bike, hung her portable speakers over the handlebars and cued up some classic Adam Ant. *Stand and Deliver* echoed around the walls as Cat peddled steadily towards the exit, the bike accompanying Cat's singing with a loud *squeak, squook, squeak, squook.*

The afternoon sun hung low in the sky and turned the sea to liquid copper. Cat didn't mind if she fished all night, though. She had her duty-free booze, a packet of French fags and Adam and the Ants Greatest Hits. What's not to like? The only problem were the pot-boiling natives. Even in her onesie, she didn't feel entirely safe, but then again, she was out at sea, so she'd have no trouble outrunning them.

She hadn't noticed the irritating squeak until now. That was probably because she was half asleep when she'd arrived, but the pedalo definitely needed oiling. *Squeak, squook, squeak, squook.* It sounded just like the old bike in the bomb shelter. Cat turned up her iPod to drown out the noise and steered a course out beyond the breaking surf.

.. Cat had a dozen fish ready for grilling and didn't care if the loud music scared the rest away. It had been a good day, but the sky was definitely turning a darker shade of storm. The bronzed horizon had now bruised to a blue-black smear, and the wind flecked the sea with cappuccino foam.

'I think,' Cat said to the bag of fish, 'it's time to go.' The gentle waves licking the pearlescent sand had disappeared behind a rolling wall of water that streamed a glowing white spume from its top. There was only one way back in and Cat knew it.

'Surf's up!' she yelled and pedaled for the next humping wave. The squeak, squook turned to a manic squeak-eek-eek-eek-eek as the pedalo plunged down the near-vertical face of the darkened wave.

The sky vanished behind the barrelling tube, and Cat found herself screaming through a brilliant blue-white crystal tunnel as lightning flashbulbed overhead.

The boom of thunder cannoned Cat out of the collapsing mouth of the wave. Squeak-eek-eek-eek-eek! She glanced over her shoulder, and a detonation of white-water filled her vision as a second lightning bolt sizzled overhead. 'Fuck a duck!' yelled Cat. 'What a rush!'

The high-octane squealing settled back into a rhythmic squeak, squook once again as Cat pedalled for the shore.

Fat splats of rain darkened the white sand as Cat hauled the little craft up beyond the high-water mark. Cat looked up at the sky and nodded. She'd better get under cover before the storm made landfall, and besides, she had fish to fry.

Cat leaned back in the antique deckchair and burped. Finding a working gas grill was a proper result! This place had it all, except for, maybe, a fridge full of beer.

The storm had landed with a bang, but all Cat could hear was a faint screaming as the wind blew across the entrance up at the surface.

She burped again, stretched and yawned. There was no point getting bored as there were probably miles of tunnels to explore. Hooking the loudspeakers to the bike again, she squeaked and squooked her way deeper into the earth.

She howled along with the music as she pedaled on. It had reached her favourite part about *soul* and *conscience*. She always found that part to be kind of mystical, and it made her want to sing even louder. Her voice bounced down the hard concrete tunnel, returning half a second later as tuneless garble.

The deeper she went, the darker it became, as working lightbulbs became increasingly scarce, then rare, then non-existent.

Cat's pupils expanded to capture the meanest of glimmers but even then, she nearly missed the metal ladder bolted to the wall. 'Whoa there. Hold up!' She skidded to a juddering stop and looked up into a darkness so thick, she could almost scratch it.

She mounted the flaking steps and soon came to a rusted steel hatch with a long handle. The lever had been well greased and looked in pretty good condition, considering its age. She gripped the handle and pushed. It unlocked with a satisfying clunk.

Pineapple and mango. Cat sniffed the air again. It was definitely pineapple and mango. The scent drifting into the tunnel also had hints of toilet cleaner and mint mouthwash. Cat frowned. What *was* this place? She eased the door up a notch and peeped out through the gap. The clean white bathroom with the black and white tiled floor looked a whole lot newer than the rest of the base. It must be a modern addition.

She opened the hatch fully and stepped out onto the bathroom floor. King-sized bath, shower, big fluffy towels. It must be the officers' quarters, or something.

Stealing out into the hallway, a lightning flash briefly revealed framed pictures of a tropical beach, and a rush mat runner that led to an open door. The rolling boom that followed, rattled the pictures before dying away to leave the shouts and cries of the hurricane as it battered the building.

Bimbling through the open door, Cat stopped and stared. 'Someone needs to clean up,' she said as she stepped around the broken glass into a kitchen that was small but well stocked. Rum, beer, sorted! Finding a bottle opener was easy and as for knives and forks, well, who needs them for barbequed chicken wings?

Contentment filled Cat with the urge to sing, and she battled to out-do the raging wind and rain as she threw some shapes on the kitchen table. She stopped singing, pretended to point a flint-lock pistol at an imaginary foe and, at full volume, demanded his money or his life. She loved playing the highwayman, just like her hero.

Hopping down off the table, she fumbled in her onesie. 'Now, where did I put those French fags?' The pink zippo shot a three-inch flame into the semi-darkness of the unlit kitchen. Smoke belched from the cigarette, filling the room with a rancid blue fog. 'Bugger me,' said Cat. 'I'll remember not to light one of these up in a confined space, again.'

She ran the cigarette under the tap before dropping the soggy dog-end into the bin. 'Better check the rest of this place out.' She opened a door on the left of the hallway and stepped into a bomb-site of a bedroom. The bedside lamp lay broken on the wooden floor, and the duvet was bunched up by the pillows. The wind screamed its annoyance from outside and a palm frond slapped against the patio door making Cat jump. Did someone just fart, or was it the storm? She scanned the room. Nothing. Deciding it must be her imagination, she looked around the bedroom one last time. As nice as the place was, it was way too noisy to sleep in whilst the hurricane was blowing.

The bike squeaked and squooked as Cat wobbled her way back down the concrete tunnel. The bottle of 12-year-old rum she had found in the kitchen cupboard had a kick that belied its smoothness.

She was about to start singing again, when

the bike bounced off the metal cabinets in the locker room tipping Cat unceremoniously onto a wooden bench. As she lay staring at the grey ceiling, an idea flashed into her head. There were old Tannoy speakers just about everywhere in this place. No doubt to warn people about an upcoming nuclear blast. If she could wire her iPod into the sound system, she would freak out any cannibals that might be out there and use it as an alarm to get herself up in the morning, as well.

…Her sound system was a success and her favourite pop star was now blasting from at least fifty Tannoy speakers.

CHAPTER 5

Ralph

'**F**antastic. Just simply fantastic. Cheers, Marvin and thanks again.' The late afternoon sun shone through the raised bottle and cast a green light across the patio table. Ralph was happy. Happier and more relaxed than he'd been in more than two years.

'No problem, man.' Marvin clinked his bottle against Ralph's, dreadlocks trailing onto his bare mahogany shoulders that almost glowed in the amber light.

'Listen, Ralph.' Marvin stood and stretched. 'I'm going out in de boat to check de lobster pots for tomorrow's barbeque. Do you fancy coming along, or are you happy just chillin'?'

Ralph leaned back on the sun lounger. He liked Marvin. Marvin was seriously laid back, and he had a really cool Caribbean accent, to boot.

'No, I'm OK. I'm going for a walk on the beach, and I might go for a swim.' Ralph smiled. It felt good being away from the hustle, the bustle, and the midas cat. Thoughts of Lauren were never far from the surface, though. Even though she had remarried, he never stopped imagining ways of winning her back.

'Hey, don't forget what I told you.' Marvin's 6-foot-4 frame eclipsed the sun as he stood in front of Ralph.

'Yeah, I know,' said Ralph. 'Don't swim off the north shore due to the dangerous currents, and the big surf that can suddenly jack up out of nowhere.'

'Dat's what I'm talkin' about. You be cool an' I'll see ya later.'

The Robinson Crusoe Experience was everything Ralph had hoped it would be and more. The *beach hut* was a luxury apartment with an outdoor jacuzzi, wi-fi, air-con and 65-inch flat screen TV. Along with Marvin's place a couple of hundred metres down the beach, it was one of only two properties on the entire island. Just him and his very own Man Friday. He slipped out of the sun lounger, drained the last of his beer and strolled along the edge of the sand, ankle deep in the warm West Indian water. So, cousin Rolph was fuming, was he? 'Am I bothered?' he said aloud and chuckled. 'Wanker!'

The warm breeze ruffling Ralph's toupee carried with it the jungle-sounds of the island. Birds sang along with the chirp of the crickets but was under-scored by a sound that barely touched the outer reaches of his hearing. *Squeak, squook, squeak, squook.* Was it coming from his apartment? He stopped, straining to catch the weird noise. Un-mistakable words flowed on the warm currents of air. They were the lyrics to *Stand and Deliver.*

Beer refluxed in Ralph's throat. 'No. It's n-not,' he stuttered. 'It's impossible.' He bent double as his vision blurred. 'There is no midas cat. There is no midas cat.' He straightened and turned to face the apartment. After a good five minutes of birdsong, rustling palm trees and little else, Ralph walked unsteadily up the beach towards the head-land.

In the distance he caught a glimpse of something reflecting the westering sun. He screwed his eyes to slits. Beyond the lapping waves was a tiny boat that looked for all the world like a pedalo. There was only him and Marvin on the island, so who the hell was that?

Squeak, squook, squeak, squook. Ralph stopped, one foot hovering above the sand. It was that weird noise again, but this time it was coming from the tiny craft. There was someone fishing from a bloody pedalo. This was something he had to see. He ran towards the headland, not taking his eyes from the little boat.

Ralph pulled up short, skidding on the wet sand. Adam and the Ants floated on the freshening breeze.

'There is no midas cat.' He squinched his eyes shut. 'There is no midas cat.' He opened them again. The sun had dipped behind an angry looking cloud, and the breeze's volume had been turned up to wind-level. The benign wavelets that tickled the shoreline had been swallowed up by a foaming soup of vicious white-water. A tropical storm was winding itself up, and out there was... the midas cat? How did it know he was here? He hadn't told anyone. Then again, the midas cat was Satan's pet, so it must know everything.

Ralph stared at the midas cat, for he was sure that was what it was. It bobbed like an empty bottle on the increasingly angry sea. The hellish creature was going to drown. Oh yes. Halle-fucking-lujah! He'd be free! But his therapist had told him there was no midas cat. If there *was* no midas cat, then what the hell was that thing out there, then?

The sky darkened to a swollen bruise, and a thunderous roar filled the air. Ralph watched transfixed as an enormous swell rolled towards the shore. It must have been a twenty-footer, maybe even bigger.

'Surf's up!' The battle-cry of a hardcore wave rider came in on the wind just as a crackling flash of lightning ripped the air. *Squeak-eek-eek-eek-eek-eek!* The creature hurtled down the face of the wave, silhouetted by the blue-white flare. The after-image that burnt itself into Ralph's retinas had pointed ears, so it *was* the midas cat, wasn't it?

The tiny boat vanished as the huge wave folded in on itself.

Ralph had stopped breathing. Nobody could survive that, surely? The explosion of thunder came a second later, followed by a red-lining *squeak-eek-eek-eek-eek-eek!* Out of the thirty-foot spume shot the pointy-eared maniac, flash-lit by a second bolt of lightning.

'No fucking way!' Ralph ran as best as he could towards the headland, his bad leg throbbing in spite of the years of physio. He had a grudging respect for whoever, or whatever, had just ridden that monster wave on a pedalo.

As he rounded the corner, he ran headlong into hard driving rain and a howling wind but no midas cat. It had vanished. It came out of the mouth of the tube and shot out of sight, but where had it gone? He was imagining things. He must be. 'There is no midas cat!' He screamed into the building gale before turning and hop-limping back towards the apartment.

'Marvin, you've got to help me!' Ralph had to yell to make himself heard. The storm had hit the nitro button and opened the dump-valves all at once.

'Wass up, man?' Marvin pulled the hood of his kagool over his head. 'Dis hurricane wasn't forecast, you know.' He took hold of Ralph's arm and led him into the apartment, sliding the patio doors shut against the raging storm. 'Sit down dere an' you tell me.' He peered from under the hood's peak. 'Are you hurt?'

Ralph flopped onto the bed and shook his head. 'No, it's nothing like that. It's just, well...' No words were adequate. His life wasn't his own anymore and it was all down to... 'The midas cat!' He almost spewed the words out. 'It's followed me here. It's haunting me. The damned thing's after my soul. I swear it!'

Marvin started pacing, his raincoat dripping fat splats onto the wooden floorboards. 'Now, what is a midas cat?'

Ralph ran through his history with the midas cat whilst Marvin paced.

'Hmm.' Marvin rubbed a hand over his stubbled chin. 'Don't worry.' He stopped moving and smiled. 'I'm a voodoo priest. Dat's no midas cat. Dat's a voodoo spirit called Lord Skcollob.'

'Do what?' Ralph's head snapped up. Was this bloke for real? Lord Skcollob? What sort of bollocks was this?

'Yeah, man. De Lord Skcollob can summon storms out of nowhere.'

The overhead light flickered and dimmed before dying completely. Ralph flinched and grabbed fistfuls of duvet as lightning lit the room with a wood-splitting boom. 'Wh-what's it look like?'

Marvin nodded slowly as if in deep thought. After what felt like an age, he spoke in a deep, low rumble. 'De Lord Skcollob is a shape shifting demon from de pits of de underworld. Nobody knows what he really looks like apart from de glowing devil eyes dat shine in de dark.'

'What else?' Under normal circumstances Ralph would have said that Marvin was full of shit. Right now, though, in the middle of a hurricane, he wasn't so sure.

'Well.' Marvin paused and stared Ralph straight in the eye. 'It appears out of a cloud of evil smelling smoke. Did you see de smoke?'

Ralph had to admit that he hadn't. 'So I'm all right, then?'

'Dat all depends on whether it's sung to you, or not.'

Ralph felt sick. It doesn't *stop* bloody singing. 'Adam Ant,' he said weakly. He was sure he saw a smile flick across Marvin's face. Was he taking the piss? Ralph couldn't be certain in the failing light.

'Ah, yes.' Marvin clicked his fingers. 'I see.'

'What?' Ralph jumped to his feet; his doubt being steadily bricked up behind a wall of convincing hokum. 'What do you see?'

'I'm going to perform a spell of protection.' He reached forwards and yanked a hair from Ralph's toupee. 'I'll need to burn dis.' He studied the hair for a long moment before speaking again. 'Just so long as de drums of death don't start, you'll be OK.'

'The what?' It just kept getting better. 'Drums of death? Do I really want to know?'

'A repetitious drumbeat that comes from de bowels of de earth.' Marvin waved his hands in front of his face as if he was casting some kind of incantation. 'You hear de drums an' you be dead in 24 hours unless you get off de island.'

A tiny sliver of doubt pierced Ralph's superstitious armour. Drums of death? Marvin had to have been making all this guff up, and as for him being a voodoo priest. Well, come on. He works for a holiday company as a glorified handyman and cleaner.

'I'm going back to my apartment now.' Marvin headed for the patio door. 'I'll perform de ritual immediately.' He smiled at Ralph. 'Trust me,' he said. 'You'll be fine.'

The restorative effects of the holiday had been ruined. 'There is no midas cat, Goddammit!' Midas cat, voodoo spirit, or Adam Ant rehearsing for an 80s comeback tour, it didn't matter to Ralph. Something was going on, and he was damned sure he was going to find out what.

Every time something weird had happened, Marvin was nowhere to be seen. Ralph's brain started connecting the dots. 'What a fucker!' Ralph opened the fridge and grabbed a beer. 'All that crap about, what was it again? Lord Skcollob? He was convinced Marvin was playing on his fears and imagination. 'Ah, such bollocks!' He took a long pull on the beer and froze.

Squeak, squook, squeak, squook. He spun around, beer splashing across the work surface. Cutting through the hurricane's squall was that noise again.

…Garbled singing floated up through the floor.

Three words cut through the distorted echoes; *soul, conscience* and *mine.*

Marvin had only just left, so it couldn't be him. If it wasn't Marvin, then...He didn't feel the bottle slip from his grasp, but the cold, malty wetness splashing up his leg slapped him into action. 'Fuck me, it's real!' Panic lit up inside him like a flare gun. 'Oh, Jesus! It's Lord Skcollob!' He headed for the bedroom. If he could get out of the patio doors before the evil spirit got to him, he could run down the beach to Marvin's place. Marvin really *was* a voodoo priest. He'd know what to do.

The sky lit up a livid purple as a stuttering flash was chased by a tearing scream of thunder. In the negative afterglow, Ralph could see an uninhabitable landscape. If he went out there, he'd die. If he stayed inside, he'd die.

A loud clunk came from the bathroom, and a warm trickle traced a path down the inside of Ralph's leg. Lord Skcollob was in the toilet. He had no choice but to hide.

Like a 4-year-old child afraid of the dark, Ralph dived under the duvet, knocking the bedside lamp to the floor with a crash.

A second lightning bolt and thunder-clap rattled the pictures in the hallway. Ralph tensed. Lord Skcollob was talking to himself. No doubt casting a voodoo spell to drag him into the underworld.

Marvin had told him that if it sung, he was

screwed. Well guess what? It *was* singing. He *was* screwed.

All of a sudden it stopped its hellish yowling. Ralph hoped that was a good thing, but in reality he knew it could only be bad. He wasn't wrong. It was yelling. It wanted either his money or his life. Ralph buried his face in the pillow and willed himself not to scream. His money or his life? He'd gladly hand over the inheritance he'd effectively stolen from cousin Rolph, but he couldn't exactly get to a bloody cash-point machine, could he?

All of this because of that poxy will. Divine retribution was a bitch! Ralph sniffed. What was it Marvin had said about evil smelling smoke? He forced himself to concentrate, but when there was a soul-sucking demon in the room next door, it was kind of hard. A pungent aroma had filtered through the pillow. Stale cigarettes and wet dog tinged with a sulphurous afterburn. It *was* the demon. Lord Skcollob, voodoo prince of the underworld always appeared in a cloud of foul-smelling smoke and had glowing eyes. *That* was what Marvin had said.

Ralph risked a look and peeped from under the duvet. What he saw almost stopped his heart.

Standing in the darkened doorway was his death sentence. A shadowy shape no taller than a 6-year-old child with iridescent silver-green eyes. If he had any doubts left at all, the glowing eyes shot them to confetti.

Ralph farted, and he sensed the demon tense.

This was it. Any second now his soul would get ripped from his body.

He scrunched his eyes shut and waited for the end.

How long he waited, he didn't know because the next thing he heard was a steady *squeak, squook, squeak, squook* that faded away, leaving nothing but the shriek of the wind outside.

He slid off the bed onto the floor and lay there panting. He was alive. The devil hadn't taken him. He laughed, the sound alien to him. He'd survived a voodoo spirit. 'Screw you, Lord Skcollob!' He tottered into the kitchen. Chicken bones were scattered across the work surface which was also covered in pawprints.

Ralph frowned. Pawprints? He was moving around the small room in a daze when Adam and the Ants exploded from everywhere at once. He hadn't got away with it. He now knew that the demon was toying with him and how much knowledge it possessed. It must have heard about the midas cat. Either that, or it *knew* the midas cat. That's it! The lightbulb moment was so vivid, it almost hurt.

He sunk to the floor, tears coursing down his face. Stand and Deliver was being delivered at a thousand decibels. The important word amongst all that din, though, was plural. It was simply *highwaymen*. Satan's pet cat and the voodoo hellspawn were in it together. The message he was being sent couldn't be clearer. He didn't stand a chance!

CHAPTER 6

Marvin

*C*aretaker wanted. Electrical, mechanical, cooking, general DIY. Interpersonal skills essential. Experience with water sports a bonus. Reply by email only: barnibrett@rce.com.

RCE: Robinson Crusoe Experience. The job of a lifetime, living for six months a year on a deserted Caribbean island. One guest only for a fortnight at a time. Meet new people, drink free beer, sail the motor cruiser. Go fishing, snorkelling, surfing, look after only one mug at a time... and get paid for it! The first three guests were stupidly rich city types. A Bentley for weekdays, the Ferrari for weekends, and the Porsche 4x4 for trips to the country and the Cheltenham Gold Cup.

That's when Marvin Pratt, Hackney native, started developing his alter ego. He liked to tell people that he was named after Marvin Gaye, but the truth wasn't quite as cool. His mother was a massive Douglas Adams fan and loved *The Hitch Hiker's Guide to the Galaxy.* She'd gone and named him after Marvin, the paranoid android. He supposed it could be worse, though. She could have named him Slartibartfast. Still, nobody need know that he was a failed second-hand car dealer in debt up to his dreadlocks to a psychotic loan shark. Especially now that he called himself Marvin Duvalier, voodoo high-priest and had dropped his cockney accent in favour of Caribbean patois, man. Add an air of mystery by hanging some chicken bones from the barby around the door. Tie a few feathers up there as well, drop in a few magical-sounding words and voila! He was no longer a back-street low-life, but a practitioner of the dark arts.

If it wasn't for the guests, the job would be absolutely perfect. Being utterly honest, though, he found most of them to be complete tossers. The women were as bad, if not worse, than the men. If he were in his late sixties, maybe he'd find a naked, oiled, 75-year-old attractive, but he was 25 and not on the market as a toy-boy.

This one was an odd fish, though. The company had told him that he used to be a banker, but he'd had some sort of breakdown. He seemed pleasant enough. Polite, quiet and reserved, but there was something that didn't entirely mesh.

'Fantastic. Just simply fantastic. Cheers, Marvin and thanks again.' Ralph raised his bottle, and the late afternoon sun caught it just right, casting an emerald glow across the tabletop.

'No problem, man.' Staying in character was much easier for Marvin than it had been at the beginning. Slipping back into his Ray Winstone was something he no longer had to worry about. He clinked his bottle against Ralph's. 'Listen, Ralph.' He stood and stretched. He had to admit, working here was certainly relaxing. If you could call it work. 'I'm going out in de boat to check de lobster pots for tomorrow's barbeque. Do you fancy coming along, or are you happy just chillin'?'

Ralph leaned back on the lounger, the sun angling through his thick wavy thatch of hair. That's when Marvin spotted the join. That syrup must have cost a few bob but even so, a syrup's a syrup, and as for the eyes, well, there was something slightly disturbing about them. They were the same colour, and that was fine. They even pointed in the same direction. The problem occurred when Ralph had sunk a few too many rum cocktails. His left eye looked as it should after a skinful, sort of bleary and unfocussed, whilst the right one stayed morning-fresh. And what about the false right foot? Something bad had happened to this week's guest. Had he been blown up, or something?

'No, I'm OK.' Ralph smiled, the crinkles at the sides of his eyes not crinkling quite enough. 'I'm going for a walk on the beach, and I might go for a swim.'

Every guest had to be warned. Marvin's induction had included an entire health and safety manual. Anything that could go wrong needed to be mentioned or the public liability insurance was void. 'Hey, don't forget what I told you.' Marvin stood directly in front of Ralph to make sure the warning sunk in.

'Yeah, I know,' said Ralph. 'Don't swim off the north shore due to the dangerous currents and the big surf that can suddenly jack up out of nowhere.'

Good, he had been listening. 'Dat's what I'm talkin' about. You be cool an' I'll see ya later.'

The storm had come out of nowhere. Lightning had ripped the sky, and the sea had become an angry, boiling mass, but he'd made it back just before it ramped up to hurricane-strength. He secured the boat to the jetty, zipped up his kagool and looked up as a manic shout cut through the screaming wind.

Marvin pulled the hood over his head and peered out from under the peek. Ralph was hop-limping up the beach, arms flailing. Had he been hurt? At least with the onset of an unforeseen hurricane, the public liability insurance was still intact.

'Dis hurricane wasn't forecast, you know.' He stared Ralph hard in the face. Undiluted terror stared back. Ralph was not OK. In fact, he was pretty fucking far from OK. He had to get him inside, away from the storm and give him the once over. The idiot better not have taken a swim off the north shore. If he had, then he was bloody lucky to be alive.

The patio door slid shut, muffling the shrieking wind. 'Sit down dere an' you tell me. Are you hurt?'

Ralph flopped onto the bed and shook his head. 'No, it's nothing like that. It's just, well...' He stared up, his eyes pointing in opposite directions. 'The midas cat!'

The words were spat out so violently, they made Marvin jump. The midas cat? What the fuck's a midas cat? Before he had a chance to digest this new word, Ralph had spewed more weirdness.

'It's followed me here. It's haunting me. The damned thing's after my soul. I swear it!'
What's followed him? What's haunting him? What in God's blue blazes was all this crap about? Marvin had to calm the maniac down and get him to talk coherently.

He paced the floor in front of Ralph as he tried to phrase the first question and concluded that there was only one way to do it. He just had to dive in. 'Now, what is a midas cat?'

The tale Ralph told him was either bullshit cubed, or he happened to be sharing an otherwise deserted island with a lunatic. A mythical talking cat that his wife wanted as a present? Whatever ganja Ralph was on, Marvin sure as hell wanted a toke. The first thing he had to do was take some of the heat out of the situation and calm the nutter. The only problem was the fact that he was not, and had never been, a social worker. He hadn't even had one. A lot of his mates at school had, but he'd been one of the lucky ones. His mum and dad never divorced, never fought. At least they never came to physical blows, at any rate, and he'd done OK at school. Quite well, actually. He wasn't like some of the knob-heads. No. He had standards. Nick a few cars, set up a dealership and buy a council house. Do things properly. It was a bloody shame that his business imploded and the *Cash-flow King* wanted to remove a digit for every week his repayments were late.

This situation, though, was a whole different ball of fur. A talking cat, what was all that about? That's when a spark of an idea ignited a blazing inferno. He was supposed to be a voodoo high-priest, so why not play up the superstitious angle? He could use magic to solve this problem.

His mind raced. If he came up with a convincing voodoo demon that he could easily *exorcise,* then Ralph would shut up about this imaginary talking cat. Tell him it was a prince of the underworld and not a, what was it again, a midas cat? He'd invent an ancient Haitian spell to use on it and abracadabra, no more midas cat. What name could he use, though? 'Hmm.' He rubbed a hand over his stubbled chin, playing for time. This was such bollocks. That was the moment a name flashed across his consciousness: Dylan Thomas. Why was that name important? His neural pathways lead him to a surprise destination. In *Under Milk Wood,* Dylan Thomas named his town *Llareggub,* which was *bugger all* spelled backwards. That was all he had to do. Spell bollocks backwards, giving him an instant demon.

'Don't worry.' He smiled in what he hoped was a reassuring manner. 'I'm a voodoo priest.' This was going to be fun. 'Dat's no midas cat. Dat's a voodoo spirit called Lord Skcollob.'

Ralph frowned. 'Do what?'

'Yeah, man.' Marvin was warming to the part he was playing. Ralph didn't have a clue that he was more Palmers Green than Caribbean. 'De Lord Skcollob can summon storms out of nowhere.'

The overhead light went bright, dim, bright and then died. Lightning tore the sky, illuminating the room with a bang. Ralph flinched, looking for all the world like he'd shat himself. 'Wh-what's it look like?'

Marvin nodded sagely. What's it look like? He was buggered if he knew, he'd only just made it up. He nodded again. Trust Ralph to ask a question he wasn't prepared for. He stared off into the middle distance, hoping he looked as though he was deep in thought, whilst he scrambled about for an idea. Of course he didn't know what it looked like. But then again, nor did Ralph, so it could look like everything and nothing. That was it! It could look like anything at all! 'De Lord Skcollob is a shape-shifting demon from de pits of de underworld. Nobody knows what he really looks like apart from de glowing devil eyes dat shine in de dark.' Marvin was especially pleased with the glowing eyes bit. It was nicely done considering he was making all of this rubbish up on the fly.

'What else?'

'Well,' said Marvin. Well indeed. He didn't have a clue what else, so he paused and stared Ralph straight in what he hoped was his real eye. Sulphurous smoke, jungle drums and siren songs. The mish-mash of myths and legends swirled in his head. It seemed his state education wasn't a complete waste, after all. Which myth to choose, though? 'It appears out of a cloud of evil smelling smoke.' This was good. 'Did you see de smoke?' Of course he didn't. It was all in the dopey git's head.

'So I'll be all right, then?'

'Dat all depends on whether it's sung to you, or not.' The old story about mermaids luring sailors to their deaths was a classic. It just kept getting better. There was no way he'd heard this creature singing.

'Adam Ant.'

Had he heard correctly? Adam ant, seriously? He stifled a grin. A talking cat from Hades that sings Adam Ant songs. Priceless! 'Ah yes.' He had to press on with the act. If he didn't, he was liable to lose it completely. 'I see.'

'What?' Ralph leapt to his feet. 'What do you see?'

'I'm going to perform a spell of protection.' Marvin reached forwards and yanked a hair from

Ralph's toupee. He'd seen it done in an old horror movie. Take something of the victim's like a lock of hair and burn it. It didn't matter if the hair wasn't actually Ralph's. It was all for show, anyway. 'I'll need to burn dis.' Add one last vital ingredient and there you have it. A perfect voodoo demon to *exorcise.* 'Just so long as de drums of death don't start, you'll be fine.'

'The what?' The last remaining bit of Ralph's tan drained away, leaving a sickly pale beige. 'Drums of death? Do I really want to know?'

Oh yes, thought Marvin. *You really do want to know.* 'A repetitious drumbeat comes from de bowels of de earth.' He made a few mysterious, black-magicky hand movements just to add a bit of spice. 'You hear de drums an' you be dead in 24 hours unless you get off de island.' Drums of death? As if! 'I'm going back to my apartment now.' Marvin headed for the patio door. 'I'll perform de ritual immediately.' He looked back at Ralph and smiled. The only ritual he was performing tonight involved a bottle of rum and a couple of sleeping tablets, so he'd be able to get a bit of shut-eye. 'You'll be fine.'

Marvin opened an eye. The sun was already riding high and cooking the apartment. He dragged himself out of bed and yanked the curtain across the picture window. The rum and nytol cocktail was certainly effective. The hangover was something special, though. If someone had dropped a damp duvet over his head and then pounded him on the back of the skull with a wooden mallet they'd replicate it almost perfectly.

He grabbed a coke from the fridge. The power was still out, and that meant firing up the generator. Not before he'd checked on Ralph, though.

The storm had destroyed the jetty, and the boat sat half on the beach and half in the jacuzzi. At least he couldn't be blamed for not tying the cruiser off properly. A large chunk of pier stuck out of the sand, still tethered securely to the craft's bow. The boat was truly screwed, so how they were getting back to the mainland was anybody's guess.

'Ralph, are you OK?' He eased open the front door and glanced towards the kitchen. 'What the hell?' Chicken bones were everywhere. As he moved in to get a better look, he spotted an unruly pattern of dirty splodges that may or may not have been pawprints. This imaginary cat was starting to become a bit too real.

A muffled chanting came from the bedroom. The same phrase over and over again. 'Ralph?' This wasn't good. Marvin sprinted up the short corridor and slammed through the door. Ralph sat on the floor; a corner of the pillow stuffed in his mouth.

'Lobshklob, myshcat. Lobshklob, myshcat.' As Marvin gently removed the pillow, the chanting became clearer. 'Lord Skcollob, midas cat. Lord

Skcollob, midas cat.'

The wheels had come off fully this time, and it was partly his fault. What had he been thinking, telling Ralph about a voodoo spirit? 'Come on, mate. On yer feet.' He'd dropped the Caribbean accent. Well, there wasn't any point now, was there? 'Let's get you back to my place and sort you out, eh? I'll get the power on and make us both a nice cuppa.'

The generator chugged rhythmically, feeding power to the kettle that had come to the boil. 'What happened last night?' Marvin sipped his tea, waiting patiently for Ralph to compose himself.

Ralph looked at Marvin over the rim of his mug, one eye focussed, the other staring off over Marvin's shoulder. 'I saw it. Lord Skcollob. It was just like you said.'

Marvin frowned. Just like he'd said? The whole story was a total crock, made up on the spot. 'Wh, what did you see?' This was fifty shades of wrong. How could he have seen a make-believe creature?

'The smoke, the eyes and the messages.'

'Messages?' Marvin had to hear this. 'What messages?'

'Adam Ant songs. It sends me coded messages in them.

Oh, good grief! He really had lost the plot. 'Listen. This here Lord Skcollob. It... well... Look, I made it all up, just so I could exorcise it, and then you'd think it was gone. I'm no more a voodoo priest than I am an astronaut. Don't you get it? Sk-collob is bollocks spelled backwards.'

'No!' Ralph was on his feet, tea splashing across the kitchen worktop. 'I know what I saw and heard! And besides, where did those pawprints come from?

'Yeah, OK.' Marvin had to admit, the smudges did look cat-like, but he couldn't be completely certain. 'I'll tell you what. Let's go back to your place and have a look around together.'

'Sure,' said Ralph. 'I'd like that.'

CHAPTER 7

The Cat

C at stretched, yawned and shook her whiskers. Having your very own 80s revival party in a cold-war nuclear bunker was pretty cool, but even Prince Charming needed sustenance. Cat's stomach growled. Ridicule may be nothing to be scared of but going without breakfast certainly was. She rummaged in her onesie. Three empty hipflasks, a packet of French fags and a pink zippo does not constitute breakfast. A trip to the surface was called for, and if Cat was on the lookout for breakfast, you could bet the cannibals were, as well. She'd just have to be extra-vigilant.

She hopped aboard the rusty bicycle and wobbled her way through the concrete tunnels.

Squeak, squook. Squeak, squook. Now she was familiar with the layout, finding the emergency escape hatch was a doddle. The latch opened easily and as she pushed up into the bathroom, fragrant scents of pineapple, mango and toothpaste drifted on a warm breeze.

The storm had blown itself out, leaving a gloriously hazy day for Cat to enjoy. All she had to do was keep an eye out for spear-wielding natives carrying a big pot and all would be well. First of all, though, some music to go with the breakfast hunting expedition. She patted herself down. No iPod. Where had she left it? She needed some music. She needed a foraging soundtrack. 'Oh yes, I remember,' she said to the empty kitchen. 'It's still plumbed into the tannoy system.' Not only was it wired to every loudspeaker in the bunker, it was also set as an alarm clock to wake Cat up in case she overslept. That meant any minute now, *Ant Music* would kick in at full volume. She'd woken before it went off and had forgotten to disarm it. Never mind, though. It'll give the natives a proper scare.

Corn on the cob, the rest of the chicken wings and a cold beer. Now that's a nutritious breakfast. None of that shredded cardboard nonsense. Cat burped, pleased with her successful hunt. Now it was time to check the rest of the place out.

The bedroom was a blaze of light as the early morning sun slanted in through the patio doors. She ambled over to the window. A motorboat stuck out of the jacuzzi, its back half resting on the edge of the sand. That was one hell of a storm last night. It was lucky the place was still in one piece. Pilings from the jetty stood like wooden soldiers above the clear turquoise sea, and assorted flotsam lay strewn across the beach.

Cat returned to her hunt, eager to discover what was in the bedside cabinet. The sun dipped behind a passing cloud as she knelt down beside the bed.

The drawer slid out silently, revealing a half pint bottle of vintage rum. 'Oh yes, the Caribbean's finest.' She pocketed the bottle, pulled out her cigarettes and spun the zippo's wheel. Time for a fag.

Thick blue smoke belched from the flaring cherry and quickly filled the room with a mix of old socks, stale farts and sewer gas. She'd forgotten how rancid the damned fags were. She stood just as the sun broke through the clouds, lighting the toxic fug a weird iridescent blue-grey. Swirls of orangey-brown weaved a trippy hypnotic pattern in the venomous haze. *Urgh,* thought Cat, *nasty.* It was at that exact moment a familiar drumbeat kicked in. Rimshots echoed through the fog followed by a heavy Burundi beat. Cat knew she was a good singer as she belted out the opening line to Ant Music. God, this was a good song! The track clicked off just before the lyrics started and *Ant Music* began from the top once again. When it restarted a third time, she knew her iPod was buggered. *That's just typical,* thought Cat and froze.

The indistinct shape of two men, backlit in the swirling fag smoke, stopped all thoughts of a broken iPod. She hadn't seen a soul since arriving on the island. The nuclear bunker had been abandoned, sure, but the report that had been left behind about the cannibalistic natives said it all. No bloody wonder the base had been abandoned!

She stared through the fetid smoke, trying to get an accurate fix on the two men. The smaller of the two was jumping up and down and, in a high-pitched keening wail, was screaming about the drums of death, whilst the one with the big hair was yelling about something called Lord Skcollob. This was some sort of voodoo jiggery-pokery and Cat wanted no part of it.

She dived for the patio door, praying to whatever deity might be listening that it was unlocked. If it wasn't, she dreaded to think what might happen. Her paw closed around the handle, and she pulled. It wasn't locked! She didn't have time to feel any relief, though. There were a couple of cannibals to escape from. She wrenched it open and looked over her shoulder just before hurtling out into the sunshine. The two men had vanished. They'd disappeared just like magic. Magic! They must have called up a voodoo spirit called Lord Skcollob by using the drums of death. She was so out of there!

She shot past the jacuzzi with the boat in it, skipped over the assorted wreckage littering the sand and ran down to the surf line. She sped up the beach without another backward glance. She could deal with most things, but supernatural beings from beyond the veil was not most things.

As she slowed to a jog, she caught sight of something flitting from tree to tree at the jungle's edge. Dropping to a walking pace, she stared into the greenery. There it was again. Thankfully it was neither a cannibal nor a voodoo death-spirit. A man in shorts and a tee-shirt peered out from behind a palm tree at Cat, and he looked terrified. Had he been on the island all along? Maybe he'd been terrorised by the same natives that were back at the beach hut thingy. Poor sod. He looked like he could do with some help. 'Hold up!' Cat yelled and scooted towards the trees.

The man took off with a hopping, limping sort of run. As Cat drew closer, the man's features became clearer. It was the idiot from the airport that hung around in shop doorways annoying clowns. *Bloody stupid thing to do if you ask me,* thought Cat as she gained on the idiot. *Now the moron's gone and got himself tangled up with voodoo cannibals.*

'Keep away from me!' The idiot screamed at something over Cat's shoulder, but when she looked, all she could see was a deserted beach and crystal blue water. This bloke was well messed up. 'Slow down,' said Cat. 'I can...' She never finished her sentence. *I can help you* was what she was going to say. There wasn't any point now, though, because the clown-bating moron had face-planted a palm tree and was now lying spark out on the sand.

Cat wasn't going to hang around any longer than

she had to. The idiot wasn't dead, she could see him breathing. He was on his own when it came to the natives, though. 'I'm outta here,' she said and headed for where she'd parked her pedalo.

CHAPTER 8

Marvin

The wooden side door to Ralph's apartment had been warped out of shape by the unrelenting rain the previous night, but at least the roof was still intact. That was one job that didn't need doing, thank God! There were plenty of other things to keep him occupied, though. The smashed jetty and all the debris littering the beach needed to be cleared up and God knows how he was going to get the boat out of the jacuzzi. That could take days. The most important job at the moment, however, was giving the place a thorough going-over.

'I think we should start in the kitchen,' said Ralph as he pulled the door open with a screech. 'That's where most of the clues are.'

Chicken bones were strewn about the tiny space

along with two well chewed corn cobs and an empty beer bottle. Whatever the hell this thing was, it sure had a healthy appetite.

'Look!' Ralph had become highly agitated and was pointing to indistinct splodges that covered the floor and worktop. 'Midas cat prints. I told you. Didn't I tell you? It's the bloody Anti-Christ, and it's got my number!'

'OK, mate, look...' Marvin had to calm him down before he did himself any permanent damage. Ralph bounced on his heels, his face an odd pinkie-purple. It looked like he was on the verge of blowing a mental gasket. 'There's obviously a rational explanation to all this.' That may have been true but what the hell it was, he didn't have the first clue. 'OK, this island's full of wildlife, yeah?'

Ralph nodded.

'We've got parrots, lizards and tree frogs. But most importantly, we've got monkeys.'

'And monkeys sing Adam Ant songs and drink beer, do they?'

Ralph had a point. That last statement had sent Marvin's mind to places he didn't want it to go. There *was* something going on here, and it wasn't a drunken 80s primate. 'Let's check out the bedroom. See if we can find any more clues.'

One of the few clouds in the clear blue vault scudded across the sun, throwing the bedroom into shadow. Evidence of Ralph's disturbed night was everywhere, from the chewed pillow to the puddle of piss. Yep, the poor bugger sure had a bad one, all right. The only thing that wasn't there, was any clue about the creature.

That's when an unearthly mist started to rise from the far side of the bed. Thick blue smoke belched from beside the bedside cabinet, filling the room with a noxious odour. Old socks, stale farts and blocked drains. Marvin's brain locked up. Lord Skcollob appearing out of a foul-smelling fog? He'd made it up, hadn't he? He was sure he'd made it up. All of that crap about the smoke and glowing devil eyes was a complete bag of well-rotted manure.

A single ray of sun lasered through the patio doors, and the spreading smoke shimmered a weird glowing blue-grey. Swirls of orangey-brown twisted in the clouds as a pair of shining green eyes lit up from deep within the toxic mist.

Glowing... devil... oh, holy fuck... eyes. It's real! Marvin felt an uncontrolled fart squeak past.

T-tap, t-tap, t-tap, t-tap, t-tap... The beginnings of a drumbeat echoed around the walls, quickly deepening to a driving rhythm. The drums of death? That was bullshit, too. It was, wasn't it? He took a step towards the door. What had he done? Had he accidentally summoned an evil spirit? The thought ran on a loop around his brain until a horrendous wailing rose from deep within the fog.

Lord Skcollob was singing. What did that mean again? He tried to pry the memory loose, but when a demon from the wrong side of the River

Styx was screeching *Ant Music* at you, it was kind of difficult to concentrate.

Liquid screaming came from Ralph, words punching through that may have been *the drums of death*, but he couldn't be entirely sure.

'It's Lord Skcollob, Lord Skcollob, Lord Skcollob!' An increasingly urgent yelling that sounded like his own voice over-rode Ralph's terror. As Marvin turned towards the bedroom door, he could see Ralph's back disappearing down the hallway. The bloody coward was running away without him. He put on a spurt and burst through the wooden side door just in time to see Ralph hop-limping as fast as he could up the beach.

Yeah, let him go. The pillock doesn't know the island like I do. He sprinted for the generator shed as hard as he could, pulled open the door and dived inside. The door clapped shut. He was out of sight, unlike Ralph.

With no communications and no transport off the island, though, it was only a matter of time before Lord Skcollob found him. How long could anybody hide from a demon? He leaned back, closed his eyes and waited for the end.

CHAPTER 9

Ralph

'I saw it.' The image of the demon had taken up permanent residence inside Ralph's head. 'Lord Skcollob. It was just like you said.'

Marvin frowned. 'Wh-what did you see?'

'The smoke, the eyes and the messages.' The devil's helper had been communicating with him. It had told him it was working with the damned midas cat. Why would it lie about a thing like that?

'Messages?' Marvin straightened up. 'What messages?'

'Adam Ant songs. It sends me coded messages in them.'

'Listen,' said Marvin, all trace of the Caribbean accent wiped away by the cockney twang. 'This here Lord Skcollob.' He paused as if searching for the right words. 'It, well… Look, I made it all up, just so I could *exorcise* it, and then you'd think it was gone.'

That wasn't right. It couldn't be. If Lord Skcollob wasn't real, then neither was the midas cat. That sodding shrink and all his *there is no midas cat* crap. He'd seen the damned thing!

'I'm no more a voodoo priest than I am an astronaut. Don't you get it?' said Marvin.
Get it? Get what? Ralph felt his grip on the conversation slip dangerously. What the hell was Marvin banging on about?

'Skcollob is bollocks.' Marvin held out his hands as if revealing how a magic trick was performed. Lord Skcollob was definitely not bollocks. He'd not only seen it; he'd heard and smelled it.

Marvin shook his head. 'Skcollob is bollocks spelled backwards.'
Ralph tried but couldn't accept the fact that he'd been duped. What about the apparition and the music? 'No!' He leapt to his feet, tea splattering across the work surface. 'I know what I saw and heard!' He hadn't imagined a whole night of Adam Ant coming up through the floor from the pits of hell. 'And besides, where did the pawprints come from?'

'Yeah, OK.' Marvin paused as if weighing the situation up. 'I tell you what,' he said, 'let's go back to your place and have a look around together.'

'Sure,' said Ralph. 'I'd like that.'

Ralph heaved open the warped door with a screech. Going in through the side entrance should have been a good idea. Sneak up on the monster and its pet. The scream of swollen joinery had destroyed any element of surprise, though. 'I think we should start in the kitchen. That's where most of the clues are.'

The clues were the remains of a midnight feast. Chicken bones, corn cobs, and an empty beer bottle lay scattered around the tiny room, but in amongst the rubbish were what looked like pawprints. 'Look!' He pointed to the dirty splodges. 'Midas cat prints. I told you. Didn't I tell you?' That sealed it. His therapist was so fired! Now he had proof of the cat's existence, he'd sue the self-righteous prick into the bargain! 'It's the bloody Anti-Christ, and it's got my number!' Tremors turned to an uncontrollable shaking, and his pulse throbbed in his temples. He was being tracked down by a satanic hell-dweller and its owner.

'OK, mate, look...' Marvin spoke in what Ralph took to be a soothing voice. The midas cat had been in his kitchen, and a voodoo death-spirit had stalked into his bedroom whilst he hid under the duvet. No, he didn't feel like being soothed right now.

'There's obviously a rational explanation to all this.' Marvin was off on his calming rap once again, but Ralph was having none of it. If there was a rational explanation, he sure as shit wanted to hear it!

'OK,' said Marvin, 'this island's full of wildlife, yeah?'

Too bloody wild, thought Ralph and nodded.

'We've got parrots, lizards, tree frogs but most importantly, we've got monkeys.'

Christ on a pedalo, was that his theory? 'And monkeys sing Adam Ant songs and drink beer, do they?' He stared pointedly at Marvin knowing full well that he didn't have a comeback.

'Let's check out the bedroom. See if we can find any more clues,' said Marvin.

When the sun dipped behind a cloud and shadowed the room, it gave Ralph an involuntary shiver. Memories of the previous night's visit and unrelenting pounding music crashed through his flimsy mental defences. Things are supposed to look better in the daylight, but he wasn't so sure as a billowing pall of smoke rose from behind the bed. Stale farts and toe-jam with a bass-note of clogged sewers attacked his senses as the malodourous fog quickly filled the room.

He would have prayed if he thought it would do any good, but all thoughts of prayer evaporated as the sun shot a targeted ray into the room. The preternatural mist turned a pale bluey-grey with twists of orangey-brown weaving through it. Pray? All he could do was stare as two huge green eyes lit up from deep within the rising hell-mist.

Somebody farted. It must have been a signal for

the drums of death. T-tap, t-tap, t-tap, t-tap, t-tap... A death-watch rhythm filtered up from beneath the floor joined by a heavier backbeat.

The demon broke into song. The drums of death? It was the intro to *Ant Music.* A voodoo arch-devil uses *Ant Music* as his theme tune? The fucking irony!

The midas cat, the demon and Adam Ant. The unholy trinity! Ralph's brain bypassed its safety valve, redlined and went into full mental meltdown. Liquid wailing was punctuated by screams of *the drums of death!* It may have been his own screaming, but he neither knew nor cared. With no prompting from his brain, his feet propelled him out of the room and down the hall.

The soft white sand would, under normal circumstances, have been difficult to run on whilst wearing sandals. The adrenaline screaming through Ralph's veins, though, pushed his fear-wracked body stumbling on towards the tree line.

He had to get away from Lord Whatever-the-hell-his-name-was and find somewhere safe to hide. Having his soul ripped out by an occupant of Hades wasn't on today's to-do list.

He hadn't realised how hot the day had become until he reached the shade at the jungle's edge. Cool green light filtered through the palm fronds high above and dappled the sand with stabs of brightness. The only problem now was, should he go into the dense undergrowth and risk getting hopelessly lost and slowly starving to death? Or should he flit from tree to tree at the edge of the beach and risk a painful soul-wrenching death at the hands of Lord Skcollob and his pet cat?

He scooted as best he could to the next tree and stopped, heart ker-chunking painfully in his chest. Had he seen a flash of tabby fur down by the water's edge, or had his fear manufactured the worst case scenario? He peeped from behind the rough trunk of the palm tree. As hot as the day had become, he suddenly felt icy cold as the sweat tracking down his back suddenly turned arctic. Standing at the edge of the surf was the creature that had all but destroyed his life, and it was staring straight at him. That one thing proved his theory. Lord Skcollob was on Team Tabby and had sent the midas cat to carry out the hit.

'Hold up!'

What the hell? The creature from the 666th level of Tartarus was asking him to hold still whilst it vaporised him. What brand of idiot did it think he was?

Ralph took off along the beach, his bad leg fizzing with agony, and when he glanced over his shoulder to see if the feline from Hell was still following him, he wished he hadn't. There is no midas cat? No. He wouldn't sue his shrink when he got back. He'd have him whacked! If that wasn't a midas cat, then what was that thing chasing him? Scotch mist with whiskers? 'Keep away from me!' He ran as hard as he could, but the cat-thing was just too fast for him. He stared in horror as it zipped across the beach towards him.

'Slow down!'

His hitman was asking him to slow down. Sure. I'll paint a target on my forehead as well, shall I?

'I can...'

Ralph never heard what the cat had to say. He saw the palm tree half a second too late. The hollow thonk was followed by a searing head pain. Then everything went black.

The next few days were a complete blank, and how he got back to the UK was a total mystery.

At least he was being looked after, though. The hospital staff were kind enough, sure. But they were firm. He was to recover fully before being let out. That had been made absolutely clear to him. There was nothing physically wrong with him apart from a nasty bump on the head and some cuts and bruises. The thing was, though, it wasn't *that* sort of hospital. This was the kind of hospital with barred windows and if you made the wrong type of noises, they'd shoot you up with something beginning with a Z. No. After two years of therapy, he'd learned how to play the game. But even so, his subconscious mind was so heavily front loaded with voodoo spirits and psychotic arch-demon tabbies, he couldn't help the night terrors, so here he stayed.

At least they allowed him internet access which was far less dangerous than the TV room. Any time he wanted to change the channel, Norman, a long-term resident, would stand in front of him, his usual vacant stare focussing to laser accuracy. His voice would drop to a barely audible whisper, and he would start singing a line from Bowie's Ashes to Ashes. It wasn't Bowie, though, was it?

'Lord Skcollob says you'll fall flat, if you start messing with the midas cat.

The beard would move as if things lived in it, and he'd mutter the same phrase over and over. The midas cat. Everything came down to that bloody feline! What did it matter anyway? Daytime TV was crap, regardless of the channel.

The computer room was heavily guarded and internet access restricted to only a handful of sites like the weather and National Geographic. He was an ex-banker, though. Hacking big business used to be his bread and butter.

He glanced around the tiny institution-grey room one last time. Less of a room and more an oversized cupboard, it had just enough space for the single terminal and the two guards. One stood, propping up the barred door, so deep into his paperback that if a riot broke out, he probably wouldn't notice. The second guard sat rigidly still in his ladder-backed chair by the tiny window opposite. Ralph couldn't be entirely sure, but he had a feeling that he was asleep with his eyes open. He'd seen him do this a few times. Seemingly wide awake and snoring gently. Creepy!

He right-clicked and the entire internet planet opened up for him. There was only one place he wanted to go, though. The experiences of the island were still fresh wounds, but he needed to know. Did they really happen, or not? The usual psycho-babble had started already. *Blah, blah, no midas cat, blah fucking blah.* The doctors weren't there, so how the hell would *they* know?

The home page of *knowyourmidascat.com* didn't usually change that much due to the immense rarity of the animal. So when a flashing red notice appeared dead-centre, Ralph had to fight to act as normal as possible. Well, normal for a nut-shack, anyway. He read and re-read the notice just to be sure he wasn't seeing things. *Midas cat's long-lost twin sister sighted. For details and pictures, click on the link below.*

There was another one? If he tracked it down he could either sell it or use it to get Lauren back. His hands shook so violently, he miss-clicked twice, landing on an S and M site. He'd usually spend some time there, re-living his days at the club but not today. Today he had more important places to be.

'Holy fucking Christ on a pedalo!' He slapped a hand across his mouth and glanced at the guards. Thankfully the lazy bastards hadn't noticed his outburst. He'd have to be more careful, though.

When he clicked on the link, a full colour picture filled the screen. It looked like his midas cat, only slightly taller and with different markings.

The Dolly Parton wig, the can of Special Brew and the fag smouldering from the end of the cigarette holder. It was real. This time, though, before stumbling blindly into the path of the furry freight train, he'd be better prepared.

He studied the picture carefully. It had been taken from an angle and was blurred as if the photographer was moving. He enlarged a section of it and moved in closer to the screen. The wall behind the animal was spattered with blood. Wherever there's a midas cat, there's pain and suffering. That was something he knew pretty much everything about. He was an expert, and he'd use his expertise to his advantage this time around. He was about to close down the computer when he noticed the link. In his excitement, he'd nearly missed it. He clicked on the icon. It was an advert. He read it and felt the oxygen get sucked from the room. He was going to faint if he didn't at least try to breathe. Pinpricks of white light fizzed at the edge of his vision. Redemption was writ large on the monitor and all he had to do was escape.

CHAPTER 10

Rolph

Three million. He could have been retired by now. He could have been playing endless rounds of golf instead of driving a thousand miles a day for minimum wage. He'd told everyone that RW Deliveries was his own company, but of course it wasn't. Roger Weiss would probably sue him if he ever found out, but he couldn't change his story now, could he?

The over-extended unaffordable mortgage on the Mc Mansion and the leased Ferrari in the drive were all there for show. All there to prove that he was a self-made man just like his dad, who wouldn't lend him a penny. 'I dragged myself up from the gutter and so can you,' was what Dad had said. 'Prove to me that you can make it on your own and I'll write you back into my will.'

That was the catalyst that started the fake life.

He'd conned his way into a thin veneer of the high-flying company boss, and it had cost him. He'd start a new credit card, just so he could pay off the previous maxed-out loan. He'd even taken another job. Babysitting wasn't a proper job, but every penny keeping his creditors happy was a penny towards the big pay-off.

When his dad was run over and killed chasing some kid dressed as that 80s popstar, Adam Ant, he knew his time had come. The money was his. His until the will was read out, anyway. It had to be a typo, surely? Why would his dad give three million to that fucking tramp, Ralph?

Still, he had a plan. It was a damned good plan, and not only would he get his money, he'd get a fat helping of sweet revenge.

He ran his tongue over the empty gums where his front teeth used to be and absently rubbed at his black eye. The first part of the plan had gone so well until...

It was Lauren who gave him the idea in the first place. On the face of it, it was bloody brilliant. She hated the scum-sucking bottom feeder almost as much as he did. Ralph hadn't got her the birthday present she'd asked for, and when she'd searched his laptop, looking for evidence of a suspected affair, she'd discovered what his so-called club was really about. What a fucking pervert!

She'd moved on. Ralph, on the other hand, was, apparently, still fixated on some mythical talking cat. She'd given Rolph the website, and all the info that the papers weren't allowed to print. So that's what happened to Lord Lucan!

After a period of intense study, an idea germinated and started to grow. It involved his next door neighbour's 8-year-old son, Liam, a tabby onesie, some creative make-up and a digital camera.

'OK, Liam.' Rolph pushed the lit cigarette into the holder. The website had all the details needed to create the perfect midas cat. 'Are you ready?'

'Yeah.' Liam stepped from the bedroom, stumbling on the knock-off Jimmy Choos. 'But what's with this stupid wig? And I ain't wearing no girlie shoes neither.' He glared at Rolph through the cat-face make up. 'What do you want with pictures of me in this get-up, anyway?' His frown deepened, making him look like an angry kitten in a Dolly Parton outfit. 'Are you some sort of nonce? My dad puts people like you in prison.'

Rolph had nannied Liam Stone since he was a year old, and the evil kid hadn't improved with age. The nasty little bastard needed to be taught a lesson. Hanging him by his ankles from the upstairs window ought to do the trick, but if DCI Frank Stone, head of the Met's Flying Squad, caught him, he'd be the one dangling twenty feet up in the air.

Contacting Lauren, an up and coming Hollywood starlet, had been easier than convincing Liam *Lucifer* Stone to put on a pair of high heels.

Letting him keep the whole pack of Bensons had been a good start. He wasn't sure about the six-pack of Special Brew, though, but the little shit had pushed for it along with fifty quid in cash, or he'd tell his dad.

Blackmail came easy to the nasty little runt. Liam would grass him up if he didn't get fags, booze and cash, but if Frank found the stash, what would Liam tell him? *It's all down to me Dad? As if! It was Rolph, the perv from next door. He made me dress up in high heels, so he could take photos of me. This lot was to keep me quiet.* Still, it was worth the risk. Once he got his inheritance back from Ralph, he'd never have to see Liam or Frank ever again.

'OK, Liam. If I make it a round hundred, would you wear the wig and shoes? Don't worry, though, nobody will know it's you once I've Done a bit of CGI on it.'

Liam picked his nose. He did that when he was thinking. The thought must have been a complicated one because he was rummaging about as if he was prospecting for oil. Rolph wouldn't have been surprised if he didn't see anti-fracking protesters outside the window.

'Yeah. OK. I'll do it for a hundred, the fags and the beer.'

Great! Once he'd got some snaps, he could move onto stage two. 'Right, stand there and pretend to take a swig from the...' Pain zagged through his face as his nose exploded in a spray of blood, the room blurring as he flew sideways. His finger jerked down on the camera's shutter button as red splats patterned the pale-yellow wall opposite with an abstract artwork.

'What do you think you're doing, you fucking ponce?'

It was Frank. What the hell was he doing home so early? He and Valerie were supposed to be at the police department's annual ball until at least midnight. His entire plan was in serious danger of disappearing into a world of police brutality.

'Leave him, Frank!' It was Mrs Stone. Rolph had always fancied Valerie, but he knew that if he told anyone, Frank would find out and extract his teeth... via his arse.

'Get up!' Valerie dragged him upright. At least with her between him and Frank, he'd have a chance of survival that was maybe evens.

'I'm gonna...' Frank didn't finish his sentence.

'Leave it, Frank!' She still held Rolph's shirt-front in a bunched fist. 'I think you'd better leave,' she said, voice thick with anger.

'I can explain.' Rolph knew he'd said the wrong thing almost immediately. Valerie let go of his blood-spattered shirt, and in one well practiced move, landed a stinging right hook to his cheek and a straight-armed left that caved his face in from the nose down.

That had been a week ago, and as he drove to his next delivery, he smiled in spite of the broken nose and missing front teeth. The picture and advert had been uploaded and all he had to do now was wait.

Domesticated midas cat for sale. Bargain at £3,000,000. Long lost sister of the wild lesser-spotted midas cat. Not as rare as the wild breed but still highly sought after. Ideal companion for the elderly.

The game had begun...